An old friend . . .

"Why don't you just call Lila and ask her if you can borrow her video camera?" Elizabeth asked, sounding frustrated. "It doesn't have to be a big deal."

But it *was* a big deal. Lila and I used to be best friends. Now that we barely spoke, it made the idea of actually asking to borrow something from her feel totally weird.

"I don't know," Bethel chimed in as she shifted in her seat. "I don't trust that girl as far as I can throw her . . ."

"Lila's not that bad," I said, taking a deep breath. "She's just . . . unique."

"Well, let me go on record as saying I think it's a bad idea," Bethel said, looking as if she was about to give in. "If she tries to get involved—"

"She won't," I said, even though I was sure that when there was a camera around, Lila would find a way to get herself in front of it. She and I were alike in that way, at least.

"It's your call," Bethel said, lifting one shoulder.

I reached over, picked up the Princess phone from the table by the couch, and dialed the number I still knew by heart. It wasn't until it started ringing that I realized I was holding my breath.

Don't miss any of the books in SWEET VALLEY JUNIOR HIGH, an exciting series from Bantam Books!

Sweet Valley Jr. High

She's Back....

Written by
Jamie Suzanne

Created by
FRANCINE PASCAL

BANTAM BOOKS
NEW YORK · TORONTO · LONDON · SYDNEY · AUCKLAND

RL 4, 008–012

SHE'S BACK . . .

A Bantam Book / March 2001

Sweet Valley Junior High is a trademark of Francine Pascal.
Conceived by Francine Pascal.
Cover photography by Michael Segal.

Copyright © 2001 by Francine Pascal.
Cover art copyright © 2001 by 17th Street Productions,
an Alloy Online, Inc. company.

 Produced by 17th Street Productions,
an Alloy Online, Inc. company.
33 West 17th Street
New York, NY 10011.

ISBN: 0-553-48729-9

Visit us on the Web! www.randomhouse.com/kids

Published simultaneously in the United States and Canada

Bantam Books is an imprint of Random House Children's Books, a
division of Random House, Inc. BANTAM BOOKS and the rooster
colophon are registered trademarks of Random House, Inc. Bantam Books,
1540 Broadway, New York, New York 10036.

PRINTED IN THE UNITED STATES OF AMERICA

OPM   0 9 8 7 6 5 4 3 2 1

To Kacey Michelle Cotton

Lila's Journal

Yippee. Another slumber party. I'm so excited, I can hardly speak.

Yeah, right.

Sure, slumber parties used to be fun . . . when we didn't have one practically every single week! I mean, it's always the same. Set up sleeping bags, gossip, order pizza, gossip, eat pizza, gossip, watch bad movie, eat junk food, make a couple of prank calls, and then gossip until you fall asleep. Not that I don't love a good slam fest, but how many times can you discuss the fact that Mandy's love note to Bobby was picked up by John by mistake and now the class dork thinks one of the coolest girls in school is in love with him? Then the next morning the hostess's parents always present some elaborate breakfast, unashamedly trying to outdo the parents from the week before, and we all go home feeling so stuffed, we just want to go back to sleep.

Why can't we do something sophisticated for a change . . . like go out to dinner, or see a show in LA, or have a catered picnic in the park or something?

Well, whatever; I guess I should get going. If I don't get to Ashlee's house soon, I might miss Maree's reenactment of Mandy's reaction when John told her he liked her too. I mean, I really want to see it . . . *again*.

Jessica's Journal

Tonight is going to be so much fun! Liz and I are throwing a slumber party, and everybody's coming. Well, not <u>everybody</u>, everybody. What I mean is, my good friends and Liz's good friends are all going to be here—Bethel, Kristin, Anna, and Larissa.

Normally I would say another slumber party would be bo-<u>ring</u>. We've only been having them since, like, the second grade. But this one's going to be different. Kristin and Bethel are both awesome friends, and I'm really beginning to like Anna. I used to think she was annoying, but she's actually pretty funny. And I don't know Larissa that well, but she's from England, so she has to be cool. Plus I'm psyched for Liz to get to know my friends better.

I can't wait for everybody to get here. Who cares if it'll be another night of gossip, junk food, and bad movies? I'm sure with this crowd, it'll be interesting. I love our friends.

You know, I'm really glad we came to SVJH.

Jessica

"When you watch television, and I know you do," Mr. Harriman said with a big, yellow-toothy grin, "a certain kind of commercial litters the airwaves. What industry are these commercials for?"

The entire class just stared. Some were staring at the floor, some at their desks, some at Mr. Harriman, and a couple at the backs of their eyelids. Didn't our history teacher know it was too early on Monday morning for questions? Even questions about TV?

"C'mon, people," Harriman said, leaning on my sister's front-row desk, both hands gripping the edges. I felt bad for Elizabeth, who was leaning back as far as humanly possible without being rude. I could tell she was holding her breath. No one wants to get that close to Harriman's musty clothes, but that's what you get for being a suck up and sitting in the first row. The teacher gazed across the room, waiting for a raised hand he wasn't going to get.

Jessica

"The Internet!" Mr. Harriman finally announced triumphantly, pushing himself away from Elizabeth's desk. "Dot-coms! WWWs!"

I smiled. Mr. Harriman was kinda funny when he got excited.

"And as little as ten years ago, you wouldn't have seen a single commercial for a dot-com. The Internet was nothing more than a tool for computer geniuses—a toy for innovators ahead of their time. Now it's in almost every household!"

Harriman was *really* excited. I put my hand over my mouth to cover a yawn.

"Each generation has its own unique contribution to society," Harriman continued, straightening his tweed blazer. "The world as a whole—culturally, politically, socially—is quite different than it was ten years ago."

"I bet he still didn't have hair on his head ten years ago," Lacey Frells muttered under her breath. I was sitting with my back to her, so I smirked because she couldn't see me. (Normally I wouldn't give her the satisfaction of appreciating her joke.) All the people sitting around her chuckled.

"People! I propose a little project," Harriman said, raising a finger in the air.

The chuckling stopped. The few people who

had their heads on their desks sat up straight.

"A time capsule," our teacher continued. "This project can take any form—a paper, a diorama, a model, whatever you like—as long as it documents your place in society today."

I let out a loud groan, but it was okay because the rest of the class groaned along with me. Projects are so irritating. There's too much guesswork—too little direction. You never know what a teacher is going to like and what's going to make them just knit their brows and look at you like you'd just presented an alien life-form. Actually, most teachers would probably love that.

Couldn't we just take a quiz and get it over with?

"You will be graded on your insight and your creativity," Harriman said. (Just what I thought.) "And there are no rules. You may work in pairs or groups. . . ."

This got my attention. I glanced to my left at my friend Bethel McCoy. We caught each other's eyes, and Bethel nodded. Flipping my blond hair over my shoulder, I wrote the words *Time Capsule Project* across the top of my notebook in big, pink letters. This assignment was definitely going to bring me down, but at least I'd have a partner in my misery.

Bethel

I know everyone hates projects, and I usually do too. But sitting there listening as Mr. Harriman explained about the time-capsule box his class made when they were in high school, I got to thinking.

This was a pretty cool idea.

Just imagine. Fifty years from now, students at SVJH could dig up a big box of our projects and know exactly what our lives were like today. I mean, they'd probably look at our CDs the same way we look at records, and they probably wouldn't even *know* what our books were since everything will be on computers by then.

I took out my notebook and started to scribble down some ideas. The rest of the class could moan and groan and squirm about this project, but I wanted to do a good job. This wasn't like the Egyptian pyramid I made out of sugar cubes in the sixth grade. (The one that was eventually chucked in the Dumpster after I'd spent three weeks with a permanent glue-and-sugar coating on my fingertips.) This project might actually matter to society.

"Your assignments will be due next Wednesday," Mr. Harriman said, writing the date on the board with some seriously squeaky chalk as the class groaned all over again. "That's one week from this coming Wednesday. If you're going to work in groups, I'd like to know who your partners are by tomorrow morning."

I took out a pen and wrote the due date down in my notebook. I've never been that good with deadlines, so it's always a plus if I write them down. The bell rang, and everyone pretty much flew out of the room. I put my notebook in my bag and walked up to the front with Jessica.

"Can you believe this?" Jessica said, struggling with the zipper on her backpack. "I was looking at a wide-open week of vegging out in front of the TV. No tests, no big homework assignments in the foreseeable future, and now this!" She finally got the zipper free and closed her bag violently. "I swear, it's like some teachers are psychic."

"Ahhh, don't worry about it, Wakefield," I said, holding the heavy door open as we walked through. "I think this will be fun."

Jessica looked at me like I'd just started speaking Swahili. "Okay, geekball," she said with a laugh. "If you're so excited, do you have any brilliant ideas on what we can do for this project?"

I scrunched up my face as I dodged all the students crowding the hallway. "No, not yet," I admitted. We stopped at my locker, and I started twirling the lock as Jessica leaned back against the wall with a huge sigh.

"We'd better come up with something good," she said, producing a tube of lip gloss from her bag and applying it perfectly without even looking in a mirror. "My history grade is seriously lacking." She smacked her lips together like she was punctuating her sentence. Then she rolled her eyes, which made me laugh.

I don't know what it is about Jessica. With all the eye rolling and lip-gloss smacking, you'd think she wouldn't be my type of girl. That's definitely what I thought when she first came to SVJH. I guess you could say I'm pretty no-nonsense. So when I met Jessica, I took one look at her perfect blond hair, her perfect tan, her perfectly matched outfit . . . and wrote her off as a dimwit. Then it turned out I was totally wrong. Jessica may just be the goofiest, funniest, coolest friend I've ever had.

"Don't worry about it," I told her as I pulled my math book out from under a stack of papers and notebooks. "We'll come up with something," I added confidently. "Why don't we get together after track practice today and try to figure it out?"

"Okay!" Jessica agreed, brightening a little. "You can come over to my house, and we'll pig out."

"Sounds like a plan," I said. The warning bell rang, and I slammed my locker shut.

"Later!" Jessica said, taking off down the hall.

"Later!" I called after her. Suddenly I couldn't wait to get out of school that day (not that I normally wanted to stay there for hours). This project was definitely going to be cool, but working with Jessica was going to make it even cooler.

Lila

I paid the pinched-faced lady behind
the counter at the cafeteria, picked up my tray,
and headed out into the lunchroom with my
friends, the Double E's, trailing behind me. As I
wove my way through the crowd toward our
normal table, I held my head up and my shoulders back. A person is visible to the entire
school on her walk through the cafeteria. I had
to look calm, comfortable, and at my best—even
if navigating the moving chairs and hyper people was really hard without looking at my feet.

Finally I dropped safely into one of our uncomfortable plastic chairs from, like, the seventies, and
my friends sat down all around me. Already my
thighs were sticking to the seat. So much for cute
little minidresses.

"So," I said, ripping into my little packet of
lite Italian dressing. "Did you guys *see* the outfit
Miss Crenshaw has on today? Can you say clash
nightmare?"

"I know!" Courtnee said as she plunged her

plastic fork into the pasta of the day. "I mean, who told her that pink went with—"

"That green?" Maree finished for her. "Does she own a mirror, or does she just wing it every day?"

Wait a minute, I thought, looking around at my friends' trays. *The pasta of the day?*

"What are you guys eating?" I blurted out, my stomach turning. Maree and Courtnee froze, and their faces went white as if a teacher had just caught them passing notes in class. Which had happened pretty much every day this year. But Ashlee just took a huge bite of what looked to me like slimy noodles in even slimier marinara sauce.

"It's good," Ashlee said, washing down her mouthful with a dainty sip of water. "I'm kind of sick of eating salad every day."

I looked down at my plate of semiwilted lettuce and not-so-ripe tomatoes. It wasn't overly appealing, but it was the only edible thing in the cafeteria as far as I was concerned. And besides, I always got salad, and my friends always got what I got. Ever since we'd first started hanging out, if I'd decided to live on the edge and get a root beer, Ashlee would jump right in, and the other two would follow. What was going on here?

They were all looking at me, so I knew I had to say something.

"Do what you want," I said, digging into my salad. "Just don't come running to me when your stomachs freak out later."

Maree grinned and stuffed a huge forkful of pasta into her mouth, dribbling some sauce on her chin. "You should really try it, Li," she said, her mouth full.

"I'll pass," I answered, suddenly losing the urge to eat anything at all.

"So, do you guys want to go see *Time and Time Again* after school today?" Courtnee suggested excitedly. She whipped out a crumply, ripped-off section of newspaper from her messenger bag and flattened it out on the table. "It's playing at the tenplex at four and six and the Big Mesa theater at four forty-five and—"

"Wait a second," I interrupted, pushing back from the table just a touch. "Didn't we already see that lame movie?"

"You thought it was lame?" Maree said, her brown eyes wide. "I thought it was so romantic."

"What about when Ben Affleck said, 'Nothing could separate us . . . not in this century'?" Courtnee said, deepening her voice, leaning her elbows on the table, and grabbing Ashlee's hands across their trays.

"'Do you mean it, Mick? Are you really going to stay?'" Ashlee recited dramatically, tossing her shoulder-length red hair back from her face.

It was all I could do to keep from rolling my eyes. I mean, I could have written better dialogue than that. I've heard better dialogue than that on soap operas . . . maybe.

"We totally have to see it again," Maree gushed.

Well, there was no way they were getting me to sit on my butt for another two hours and be tortured for the second time. Ben was nice to look at, but that's why we have magazines.

"I have a better idea," I said, suddenly inspired. "The new issue of *Flair* just came out, and it's their yearly makeover magazine. Why don't you guys come over to my house after school, and we'll hang out by the pool and go through it?"

I looked at each of them, smiling to try to get some enthusiasm going.

"That sounds . . . fun, right, guys?" Maree said finally, glancing at Ashlee and Courtnee.

"Yeah," Courtnee agreed, pushing her pasta around in front of her. "There's nothing better than a good makeover issue."

Ashlee sighed. I guess she really liked that stupid movie. "Okay," she said finally. "I'm in if you guys are in."

"Besides, I have been thinking about getting a haircut," Maree said, breaking into a grin. "Maybe they'll have some pictures I can use for reference."

As Ashlee and Courtnee started to play with Maree's hair and talk about layers, highlights, and bangs, I dug back into my salad, trying not to grin *too* widely.

This was more like it.

Bethel

"Maybe we could make a mix tape," I said, grabbing a carrot stick and dipping it into the bowl of ranch dressing Jessica had put out on the Wakefields' coffee table. I took a bite and leaned back into the comfy couch, my notebook on my lap. "We could tape all the different radio stations in Sweet Valley."

"Yeah, but then we're just doing music," Jessica said, doodling flowers all over the paper-bag cover on her textbook. "I don't think Harriman would accept that as a real representation of our times or whatever."

"Good point," I said, blowing a sigh at my bangs. "Okay, what else?"

Jessica dropped her pen and tossed her book aside. "I think we should just do a photo album and get it over with," she told me, stretching her arms above her head. "We could go around on our bikes and take pictures of all the most popular places in Sweet Valley and slap them in a photo album. It'll be like a little photographic tour

17

of town, and it'll take us one or two afternoons."

I frowned thoughtfully. "That's an idea." I added *photo album* to our short list of possibilities. "But I don't know. I want to think *bigger*. I just don't know how."

"A really *big* photo album?" Jessica suggested, raising her eyebrows at me.

I chucked a throw pillow at her, and it bounced off her head just as Elizabeth walked into the den. She picked up the pillow and tossed it back at me, bouncing it off my shoulder.

"Hey!" I protested.

"That's what you get for attacking my sister," Elizabeth said with a laugh. She walked over to the big chair and grabbed the remote. "Do you guys mind if I watch TV?" she asked. "*Our Best Years* is on."

"Go ahead," Jessica said with a shrug. "My brain hurts from thinking so much and coming up with nothing."

"Project issues?" Elizabeth asked as the theme song for her show started up. *Our Best Years* is a kind of documentary show that follows eight kids in a high school in New York City. Elizabeth, along with just about everyone in our entire school, is hooked. There's something about reality TV that people like. Me? I'd rather go for a run than sit in front of the "boob tube," as my dad calls it.

"What are you doing for your project?" I asked Elizabeth as I grabbed another carrot.

"Sal, Anna, and I are going to make up a Sweet Valley board game," she said, her eyes fixed on the television. "Kind of like Monopoly, you know? With the mall where Boardwalk would be and Scoops at Park Place . . ."

"That's cool," I said. Why couldn't we come up with an original idea like that?

"Yeah," Jessica added, rolling her eyes. "Leave it to the brainiacs." I laughed and immediately felt bad, but Elizabeth didn't even notice. She was mesmerized.

"Hey!" she said suddenly, causing me to jump. "Why don't you guys do a documentary? You know, of what life is like at SVJH? That would be so cool!"

I could feel my eyes light up at the suggestion, and one look at Jessica told me she was thinking the same thing. "It's perfect!" I said.

"It's even kind of trendy!" Jessica added, sitting up straight.

Documentary, I wrote in big letters across my notebook.

"Wait a second," Jessica said flatly. Uh-oh. I looked up at her, and her face had already fallen. "We don't have a video camera."

My heart dropped. "That could cause a problem."

"Well, maybe you could borrow one," Elizabeth suggested, muting the TV over a commercial and grabbing a carrot.

"Right, but who do we know with a video camera?" I said, slumping down in my seat. I tapped my pen against my notebook, thinking. "A lot of parents might have them, but they're not going to lend them out to their kids' friends."

"Yeah, what eighth-grader has their very own video camera?" Jessica lamented. She tipped back her head and stared at the ceiling like it was going to answer her.

"What about Lila?" Elizabeth said.

My stomach turned just at the sound of that name. Lila Fowler was one of Jessica's friends from her old school, but to this day I couldn't figure out why the two of them ever hung out. The one time I met Lila, she was nothing but rude with a capital *R*. She and Jessica were nothing alike.

"Yeah, right," Jessica said with a grimace. "Like I'm gonna call Lila."

"Why not?" Elizabeth asked, her brow all knitted up.

"We don't even talk anymore, Liz," Jessica said. She stared down at her lap, picking at a little stain on the front of her jeans. "I'm not going to call her out of nowhere to ask her a favor."

"But I thought you talked to her at the Manchester," Elizabeth said, referring to this club she and Jessica had gone to last week to see their friends' band play. Jessica had told me all about the show. But she hadn't told me about bumping into Lila.

"Well, I didn't really *talk* to her," Jessica replied, obviously eager to drop the topic. "I just kind of waved at her. And said hi. But that was about it."

"But Jess—"

"Nope," Jessica said, grabbing a pillow and hugging it to her chest. "There has to be a better way."

Lila

I leaned back in my favorite lounge chair out by our Olympic-size swimming pool, opened my *Flair* magazine, and sighed. The sun was warm, the breeze was perfect, and I was wearing my brand-new bathing suit Daddy had brought back for me from his last trip to the Islands. This was what I called a perfect afternoon.

"Do you think this would be a good cut for me?" Maree asked, leaning over and showing me and Ashlee a picture of Katie Holmes from some red-carpet affair.

"That would be nice," Ashlee said, glancing from the picture to Maree and back again. "You have the same bone structure as she does." Ashlee refocused her attention on her own magazine, but I almost snorted a laugh. Maree looked nothing like Katie Holmes.

"I think you should chop it all off," I said, pushing my sunglasses up to hold my hair back from my face.

Maree's hand flew to her hair, and Ashlee and Courtnee sat up so quickly, you'd think they'd just heard a gunshot. "What do you mean by 'all off'?" Maree asked, a scared look in her eyes.

"Calm down," I said. I put my magazine aside and sat up to pull her long mane of thick, plain brown hair back from her shoulders. "I'm just thinking of chin length. I'm not suggesting you shave your head." I folded her hair to chin length and held the rest back from her head. "Like this."

"What do you guys think?" Maree asked, looking at Ashlee and Courtnee with just her eyes, as if she was petrified to swivel her head.

Courtnee grabbed her bag and produced a compact mirror from the overstuffed depths in about two seconds. She opened it and handed it to Maree so she could check her reflection. Maree studied herself and frowned thoughtfully.

"It could be pretty, but it's a big change," Courtnee warned.

"Speaking of big changes," I said, grabbing my *Flair* again and flipping open to a page I had dog-eared. "Courtnee, what do you think of this?" I slapped the magazine down in front of her, and everyone leaned in to look at the page. It was an advertisement for colored contacts with all the different available shades modeled by the same girl in separate pictures.

"What do I think of what?" Courtnee said, laughing nervously.

"Those!" I said, pointing at the jade green contacts. "I think you should get them."

"Are you kidding?" Ashlee said, her voice rising about ten octaves.

I sighed and stared at her surprised face. "I'm totally serious."

"What's wrong with my eyes?" Courtnee asked, quickly fishing yet another compact out of her bag. She studied her face, pulling down on the bottom of each eye one at a time, then squinting hard at her reflection.

"They're just a little bland, that's all," I said with a shrug. "You're so pretty, Courtnee, and I think green eyes would really light up your face."

She put down the mirror and picked up the magazine, staring down at the ad warily. Everyone is nervous when they think about making a big change. Courtnee just needed a little push in the right direction, and her whole life could change for the better.

"Well, maybe . . . ," she said slowly.

"Forget it," Ashlee snapped, leaning over and flipping the magazine shut over Courtnee's finger. "Your eyes are perfect, Court," Ashlee said. She leaned back in her chair, crossed her arms, and stared out at the pristine water of the swimming pool.

For a second no one said anything. I, for one, couldn't believe Ashlee sounded so angry. She'd never used that tone before in all the time I had known her.

"Ashlee," I said, "what is your—"

But before I could finish my sentence, she glanced at her watch and grabbed her bag. "C'mon, guys," she said. "We have to get ready to go." She swung her legs over the side of her chair and shoved her feet into her little pink flip-flops.

Get ready to *go*? They'd only been here for an hour. Hester hadn't even brought out the snacks yet.

"Go where?" I asked as all my friends started to gather their things and move the lounge chairs back to where they'd been before we came outside.

"We're . . . uh . . . going to catch the four forty-five of *Time and Time Again*," Maree said, pulling her shirt on over her bathing suit. Her eyes were darting around nervously. "My mom's going to be here any second to pick us up. Are you sure you don't want to come?"

I was so stunned, I could barely even think of an answer. Of course I didn't want to go, but

25

that was not the point. I couldn't believe they'd come over here when the whole time they'd had other plans. And they hadn't even told me about it, or invited me, until this last second.

"No thanks," I said finally, managing to lean back in my chair and look casual. "I think I'll just work on my tan."

"Okay," Courtnee said. "We'll see you at school tomorrow, then."

"Bye, Lila," Maree said as she walked by my chair.

"Later," Ashlee added. And that was it. With a few flips of their flip-flops, they were gone, and I had officially been ditched.

What was going on around here?

Jessica

"What about Ronald Rheece?" I said, holding my head in my hands. "That kid has to have a video camera."

"I think his dad has one. I remember it from when he came to tape Ronald in the county spelling bee. But it's one of those old, clunky things that takes full-size tapes and has a separate microphone," Bethel said, absently twirling her pen between her fingers. "You need a cart to carry that thing around."

"No, we need to be mobile," I said, squeezing my eyes shut. I couldn't believe I was thinking about asking Ronald anyway. I didn't want to owe my geeky locker partner a favor. "Maybe we could just swipe Dad's credit card and—"

"Jess!" my sister scolded.

"Kidding!" I said, throwing my hands up in the air. "I was just kidding!"

"Why don't you just call Lila?" Elizabeth asked, sounding frustrated. "It's not like you have to be best friends with her again just because you want to borrow her camera. It doesn't have to be a big deal."

But it *was* a big deal. Lila and I used to be best friends. There was a point in life when I wouldn't have even had to ask her for something like this. I would have just gone over there, grabbed Lila's camera, and returned it when I was done. We had a mutual open-closet-and-everything-else policy. Now that we barely spoke, it made the idea of actually asking to borrow something feel totally weird.

"I'm sure she'll help you out," Elizabeth said, munching on a carrot stick like a bunny rabbit. "If only for old times' sake."

"I don't know," Bethel chimed in as she shifted in her seat. "I don't trust that girl as far as I can throw her . . . which is actually probably pretty far." Elizabeth laughed, and I chuckled halfheartedly. That second part was kind of true. Bethel is a tough, finely tuned athlete, and Lila, well, let's just say the most exercise Lila ever gets is stepping in and out of her parents' limo and on and off the escalator at the mall. I smiled at the thought.

"Lila's not that bad," I said, taking a deep breath. "She's just . . . unique." I racked my brain for an alternative, but I came up completely blank. "I hate to say it, Bethel," I added, glancing over at her. "But if we really love this idea, I don't think we have any other choice."

"All right," Bethel said reluctantly. "But let me go on record as saying I think it's a bad idea. If she tries to get involved—"

"She won't," I said, even though I was sure that when there was a camera around, Lila would find a way to get herself in front of it. She and I were alike in that way, at least.

"It's your call," Bethel said, lifting one shoulder.

I reached over, picked up the Princess phone from the table by the couch, and dialed the number I still knew by heart. It wasn't until it started ringing that I realized I was holding my breath.

Lila

For five minutes after my friends left, I just sat there in my chair, not moving a muscle. I bet I was hardly even breathing, I was so angry. My mouth was pursed into a scowl, and every time I noticed it, I relaxed my lips, but then a few seconds later I'd realize it was back in a scowl. I was very, *very* tense.

Then the cordless phone rang, startling me and causing my heart to jump. I just stared at it for a second, and then a smile spread slowly across my face. It was definitely the Double E's—most likely Ashlee calling from the cell phone her mom had just given her for her birthday. They were in the car, and Ashlee was calling to apologize for being so rude. I sat back and let it ring a few times. After the way she'd treated me in my very own backyard, there was nothing wrong with letting the girl sweat a little.

On the fourth ring I picked up the phone and hit the talk button. "Hello?" I said shortly, trying to make it sound like I was bored and not majorly annoyed.

"Lila?"

I squinted for a second. The voice on the other end of the line was familiar, but it wasn't Ashlee's.

"Jessica?" I said, confused. Why would Jessica Wakefield be calling me out of nowhere?

"Yeah . . . hey," she said. "How have you been?"

She sounded uncomfortable, but I was just happy to hear a nice voice—the voice of someone who hadn't completely dissed me in the last fifteen minutes.

"Good!" I said, forcing a cheerful tone into my voice. "What's up with you?" I leaned back on my side and started studying my nails, settling in as if I was in for a long talk. I think it was just force of habit. Jessica and I used to talk for hours on the phone every day—if we weren't hanging out together talking for hours.

"Not much," Jessica said. "Actually, I'm calling to ask a favor . . . but if you can't do it, I'll totally understand." There was a muffled sound on the other end, and I could have sworn Jessica told someone to let her talk. Must've been Elizabeth.

"What is it?" I asked, curious. We hadn't

31

talked for ages, so if she was calling me specifically to ask for something, it had to be important.

"Well, I have to make this documentary for school, like, ASAP, but I don't have a camera, and I know your dad always buys you whatever new stuff comes out at E-City, so I thought if you happened to have one, maybe you could—"

"You want my camera?" I asked, confused by her babbling.

"Yeah!" she said. "But only for a few days and it's for a good cause because we might even get on TV and—"

She cut off, and there was a muffled "ow!"

"Really?" I asked, sitting up straight as my eyebrows went up. This was interesting. And I did have the latest handheld digital camcorder just sitting in my room, collecting dust. I wouldn't mind Jessica directing a documentary on my camera—as long as I got a producing credit. Besides, it would be fun to hang out with Jessica again. Hearing her voice made me miss her a little. And hanging out with her *while* she was doing this project would give me something more interesting to do than the same old thing with the Double E's.

"So, what do you think?" Jessica asked.

"Jess," I said sweetly. "You know you can

borrow whatever you want, whenever you want. The open-closet policy didn't end when you got bused off to SVJH."

"Oh, Lila! Thank you sooo much!" Jessica gushed. There was definite joyous squealing in the background.

"No problem," I said, flicking a speck off one of my nails. "Why don't you come over after school tomorrow and we'll figure it out?"

"Sounds good," Jessica said.

"Cool!" I answered, grinning. "I can't wait to see you!"

After we hung up the phone, I lay back in my chair, tilted my face toward the sun, and smiled. This was just what I needed—a change in routine, a change in people, a change in everything. Ashlee, Courtnee, and Maree could go see *Time and Time Again* again tomorrow if they wanted. I had better things to do!

Jessica

"Wow! That was a lot easier than I thought it would be!" I said, feeling very satisfied with myself as I hung up the phone and stretched my legs out in front of me. Bethel gave me a mock-disgusted look and moved over a few inches so I didn't hit her thigh with my feet.

"I can't believe you told her it was going to be on TV!" Elizabeth was shaking her head but smiling.

Bethel and I cracked up laughing. "It was perfect!" Bethel said as we high-fived.

"Yeah, c'mon, Liz," I said, crossing my arms in front of my chest. "You know as well as I do that mentioning fame or fortune is the only way to get Lila's attention."

"I know," Elizabeth said, clicking off the TV as the end credits of her show started to roll. "But I still think she would have helped you anyway. Or at least she *should* have. You guys have been friends forever."

"Yes, and one of the reasons that friendship

34

survived for so long was because we understood each other," I told Elizabeth, grabbing a carrot and snapping off the end. "I understand how Lila works, and that is why we have a video camera." I popped the little piece of carrot into my mouth and crunched it loudly.

"All right, enough about Sweet Valley's number-one diva," Bethel said, flipping open her notebook. "Let's talk about the project. I say we focus on life at school, like Liz said. We can film Wednesday, Thursday, and Friday—"

"Oh! We can do a late practice tomorrow if I go get the camera and come right back!" I said, pulling my legs up Indian style on the couch.

"Yes!" Bethel said, writing it down. "We can go to football practice. They always run late, and you know those guys will love getting their faces on camera."

"You can each take turns bringing the camera to class," Elizabeth suggested, obviously getting caught up in our excitement.

"Good!" I said. "Then we'll get a mix of students and teachers."

"Okay, cool," Bethel said, making a note. "What else can we do?" Her brown eyes were gleaming as she brainstormed. "We can get our friends together after school a couple of days to kind of illustrate the social scene. And maybe film some family stuff this weekend."

"Great!" I said, although I didn't think my family would make for great footage—unless we wanted to tape my dad and Steven falling asleep in front of the TV like they did every single Sunday. "I'll make some phone calls tonight to make sure people are free. And we should also get behind-the-scenes stuff at school."

"Behind-the-scenes stuff?" Bethel asked, scrunching up her nose. "Behind the scenes of what?"

"Of school! You know, like, maybe we could sneak into the teachers' lounge, the janitor's office . . . maybe we could even get behind the counter at the cafeteria!" I said, suddenly feeling like I was directing an exposé on the sorry state of schools in California.

"Eeeeew!" Elizabeth and Bethel said at the same time.

"Now, that's just nasty," Bethel said.

"Yep," I agreed with a grin.

"Okay," Bethel said, scribbling a few final lines in her notebook. "So you'll go over to Lila's after school, and I'll go up to the field to talk to the guys and Coach Roth to make sure they don't mind us filming, and I'll meet you there!"

"Perfect," I said, leaning back in my seat. Not only was this the coolest project idea ever (thank you, Liz!), but Bethel was the perfect partner. This morning I'd been nothing but annoyed about this time-capsule thing, but now it seemed like it was going to be a lot of fun.

Lila

That evening I was kind of surprised none of my friends had called me yet to apologize about ditching me that afternoon. I'd been waiting to hear from them, if only to tell them about Jessica's little TV project and how I was going to be involved. Finally I figured it would be okay to call them since I did have some big news. Maybe they simply hadn't called because they were having trouble swallowing their pride.

I tried Ashlee first, but her brother said she wasn't home. After that I got both Courtnee and Maree's machines. That was weird. The movie should have ended well over an hour ago. I mean, it felt really long when I was watching it, but not *that* long. I picked up the phone one more time and dialed Ashlee's cell.

It rang a couple of times, and then Ashlee picked up. Before she even said anything, I could hear a ton of noise in the background.

"Hello?" Ashlee practically shouted, sounding giddy, as if she'd just been giggling.

"Hey, it's me," I said. Sometimes I hate cell phones. It's hard to tell if the person on the other end has even heard you.

There was a pause. "Oh . . . hey," Ashlee said. She didn't sound remorseful—just distracted.

"Where are you?" I asked, unable to keep the irritation out of my voice. I plopped down on my bed and crossed one leg over the other, staring at myself in the huge mirrored doors that lead to my closet.

"We're at Vito's!" Ashlee shouted. Apparently there was so much noise on her end, she felt the need to yell. At that moment a loud cheer erupted, and I waited for way too long before Ashlee said anything else. "Sorry," she said, laughing. "Todd just beat Ken's record. He finished four pieces of pepperoni pizza with only one glass of water."

I saw my face turn bright red in the mirror and turned away. She was at Vito's with the guys? "Who's there?" I asked, trying to keep my voice calm.

"Oh, me, Maree, Ashlee, Todd Wilkins, Ken Matthews, Aaron Dallas, some kid named Winston who just blew Sprite out of his nose." Ashlee broke into convulsive laughter, and once again I had to wait. Of course waiting gave me enough time to fume from irritation into full-blown anger. I couldn't believe they went out to dinner and didn't invite me. I mean, they could have called me when the movie ended and asked me to meet them at Vito's, right? Wasn't that just common decency? And now they were hanging out with the guys. *My* guys. The guys I had grown up with and introduced them to. I had been there when Ken had set the record Todd had apparently just broken. It was just so . . . wrong.

"So what's up?" Ashlee said finally.

What *was* up? I wondered. Why was I even on the phone with this person? Then I remembered the plan. I was going to tell her about the documentary. There was still time to save some face.

"Well, I was just calling to tell you about the extremely cool phone call I got this afternoon—"

"Omigod!" Ashlee squealed. "I can't believe you just did that!"

I sighed. "*Who* did *what?*" I demanded.

"Lila, I have to go," Ashlee said. "I can barely hear you."

"Ashlee—"

"I'll talk to you later! Bye!"

And then the line went dead. For a second I just sat there and stared at the receiver, and then I turned and slammed it down. My heart was pounding, and my chest actually hurt. This was getting old, really fast.

I lay back on my bed, took a deep breath, and closed my eyes.

What was wrong with my friends? Why was Ashlee treating me this way?

Jessica's Journal

Okay, that was weird. I was actually nervous about calling Lila. I was holding my breath while I dialed the phone. This for a girl I used to wake up with a call at 7 A.M. to ask her if she could bring her purple sandals to school so I could wear them.

It's weird how things change.

Lila and I used to talk all day, every day. I'm talking before school, after school, after dinner, between classes, <u>during</u> classes. And now I'm nervous to call her. I used to know exactly how she organized her closet (clockwise, fall to summer, divided by color within each season). I used to know how many pairs of earrings she had (eighty-seven at last count). I used to be the only other person in the world who knew where she hid the Oreo cookies so that her dad wouldn't eat them all before we got home from school (the microwave because he didn't know how to use it).

We were really close just a few months ago. Then things kind of fell apart. And I guess after a while I kind of stopped missing her.

Until now.

Elizabeth's Journal

Honestly? Even though I kept saying how sure I was that Lila would help Jessica out, I have to say, I actually wasn't so sure. I was just hoping I was right.

Why wasn't I sure? Because I'm not Lila's biggest fan. I always thought my sister's relationship with Lila was kind of one-sided. Whatever Lila wanted to do, Jessica would do. Whatever Lila wore, Jessica just had to have the same thing. Wherever Lila went on vacation, Jessica begged our parents to take us there the next year. And Lila always seemed to expect her to act that way—like a loyal follower instead of a friend.

I would have felt weird about suggesting Jessica call her at all, except that I know Jessica isn't the same person she used to be. And she'd never let Lila boss her around like that now.

At least, I hope not.

Lila

Normally I hate gym class. I don't know who it was that decided it would be a good idea for people to get all sweaty and smelly in the middle of the day and waste a perfectly good morning of grooming, but whoever it was probably had perpetual hygiene issues and wanted the rest of us to suffer as well.

But on Tuesday, as I walked out toward the soccer field on the outskirts of our normal little crowd, I couldn't be happier to be in gym. All morning I'd been uncomfortable around my friends, but how could they talk about movies or pizza or boys when we were running around kicking a little black-and-white ball?

"How funny was it last night when Matthews asked that waiter for water that was chilled, not iced?" Todd Wilkins said as we walked toward the field, tossing a soccer ball back and forth from one hand to the other. "I thought that guy was going to hit him."

"I know!" Ashlee exclaimed, tucking her

shirt into her shorts, then changing her mind and pulling it out again. The girl was always fidgeting around guys. "The poor guy was so confused."

"I felt sort of bad for him," Courtnee added unconvincingly.

I rolled my eyes and upped my pace a little. I'd only heard the story of the embarrassed waiter with the braces and the bad fashion sense about five hundred times that morning. Did we really have to go over it again? I could practically tell it myself like I'd been there. Which, of course, I hadn't been, thanks to my so-called friends.

"Hey, Lila," Aaron Dallas said, flipping his long, blond hair away from his face as he jogged to catch up with me. "Why weren't you there last night?"

I opened my mouth to snap that I hadn't been invited but immediately thought the better of it. The guys didn't have to know I'd been forgotten by my friends.

"Lila didn't want to go see the movie with us yesterday afternoon, and we went straight to Vito's from there," Ashlee piped in. I scowled. I was sort of glad she didn't make me sound like a loser, but I also didn't like the idea of someone answering my questions for me.

"I don't blame you, Lila," Todd interrupted with a laugh, passing the ball over my head to Aaron. "That *Time and Time Again* flick looks totally lame."

"I know," Aaron agreed as he juggled the ball in front of him. "Who would pay to see that . . . twice?" The guys laughed, nudging Ashlee and Courtnee, who looked beyond embarrassed. I laughed too. At least the guys agreed with me. I mean, they generally have no taste, but it's very important to Ashlee and Courtnee that the guys think they're cool. (Maree too, but she's not in my gym class.)

"Guess what, you guys?" I said, looking from Aaron to Todd, who were still walking on either side of me. "I'm seeing an old friend of ours after school today."

"Really? Who?" Todd asked.

"Jessica Wakefield," I answered with a sly grin in Aaron's direction.

"No way!" Aaron said, missing the ball for once. It came down on the side of his ankle and flew in the direction of our gym teacher, Ms. Jameson. Aaron used to have a little thing for Jessica. "Tell her I said hey," Aaron said, trying to look casual but blushing like mad.

"Man, I have to admit, I miss those Wakefield girls." Todd shook his head.

"Didn't you, like, date one of them?" Ashlee said, trying to get back into the conversation. "Leia or something?"

Todd stopped walking and looked at her. "It was Liz," he said. "And yes, she was my girl-friend."

Ashlee paled slightly at Todd's hurt tone. It wasn't her fault. She had no idea that Wilkins and Wakefield were, like, *the* couple at SVMS last year and that all this drama had constantly surrounded them. But that was kind of the point. For once that day I was in a conversation she and my other friends couldn't be involved in. Let them see if they liked how it felt.

"Want me to tell Jessica to say hi to Liz, Todd?" I asked, putting my hand on his back.

"Yeah, sure," he said, starting to walk again. "Hey, remember that time we had that class trip to that swamp reserve and you and Jessica faked sprained ankles so you wouldn't have to go on the hike?" he said, perking up again.

"Yes!" I said with a laugh. "And then we got stuck with that creepy frog-keeper woman all day while you guys went on the nature walk with the hottest guide on the planet?"

"He wasn't exactly my type, but . . . ," Aaron said.

The three of us laughed and walked ahead,

reminiscing about old times and telling stupid stories. When I glanced back, Ashlee and Courtnee were watching us, obviously annoyed, but after the way they'd treated me, I didn't care. I was starting to think Jessica Wakefield's phone call was the best thing that could have happened to me.

Jessica

When the Fowlers' maid, Hester, let me into Lila's mansion on Tuesday after school, I felt like I was stepping into a time warp. Nothing had changed. The tile floor still sparkled, the chandelier still twinkled, and the white carpet on the winding stairs was spotless. But as I climbed the familiar steps, it felt like I hadn't been there in years.

"Hey, Jess!" Lila said, meeting me at the door to her room. The minute I saw her, I relaxed. She was wearing a pair of perfectly flared jeans and the exact top I'd seen Britney Spears wearing in an interview on MTV the day before.

I gave her a hug and smiled. "Hey, Li," I said. "Great shirt."

"You like?" Lila asked, spinning so I could see the back. "I have another one if you want to borrow it. It's red—your color."

"Thanks," I said. Ah, the perks of the open-closet rule.

We went into her room, and I sat on the edge

of her huge bed. "So, what's up?" I asked as she sat down and propped the pillows up behind her.

"Not much," she answered. "The camera's over there." She lifted her chin in the direction of her vanity table, and I looked. Sitting there was a tiny camera with one of those flat-screen viewers, and it was so shiny and new, it looked like it had never been used.

"Cool," I said, looking back at Lila. "Thank you so much for letting us borrow it."

"It's really no problem," Lila said, lifting a white teddy bear and picking at its fluff. "I took out the directions too. I have no idea how the thing works."

I smirked. Not surprising. "So," I said, stretching out on my back and staring at the flowered canopy above. "How are the Double E's?"

Lila sighed. Hmmm . . . trouble in paradise? "I'm kind of bored with them, actually," she said. "They can be so . . . juvenile." She looked down at the bear and put him aside. "Aaron says hi, by the way."

My heart skipped a beat, and I returned Lila's grin. "Really?" I asked, flipping over to lie on my side and propping my head up on my hand. "How does he look?"

Jessica

"Amazing!" Lila said, leaning forward. "He grew his hair out, and he looks so . . . ugh! I can't even tell you. It's like he walked off a Coppertone bottle."

"You don't like long hair!" I exclaimed. Lila usually went for the country-club type.

"I know! But on him it works," Lila said with a satisfied little nod.

I groaned. "It's so unfair that you get to see him every day," I said, remembering last year, when Aaron and I used to pass notes to each other during science class and he would sometimes leave little messages in my locker. "Him and everyone else," I added, feeling a pang of nostalgia for my old school and friends.

"Sometimes I still can't believe that you got transferred," Lila said, plopping back into her pillows. "If you were still at Sweet Valley Middle, we'd be ruling the school right now, just like we always said we would."

I grinned. I know it sounds silly, but I felt kind of proud when Lila said that. We used to be the coolest girls in school, and we knew it. Back then I always had this confident feeling, and I kind of missed it now. Things could have been so different. If I was still at SVMS, I'd have no Lacey to deal with, and Aaron would be hanging out by my locker every day. . . .

But you have Damon, I reminded myself with a smile. My boyfriend, Damon Ross, was way more appealing than Aaron, new hair or not.

"So, can I be in your documentary?" Lila asked suddenly, breaking into my daydream.

I hesitated. I knew if Bethel were here right now, she would just say no. Flat out. "I don't know, Li," I said, trying to think of a way to get around it.

"C'mon, Jess, it would be so much fun!" she said, flipping her long, brown hair over her shoulder. Her brown eyes were sparkling with excitement, and I could just imagine what she was thinking—a star was about to be born. "You and me . . . on the prowl. It would be just like old times," Lila added.

"Well, I do have this project partner . . . ," I said. "And it's supposed to be about life at SVJH. . . ."

"Right, but it's *my* camera," Lila said, crossing her arms over her chest and getting that won't-take-no-for-an-answer look on her face that I knew all too well. "I mean, it's only fair."

I rolled my eyes at her but smiled. Lila was still Lila. "Okay," I said finally. "I'm sure we can work you in somehow."

"Yay!" Lila squealed, clapping and leaning forward to hug me. "This is going to be so much fun."

Jessica

I hugged her back, squeezing my eyes shut and grinning. I hadn't realized how much I missed Lila, and I was glad she was going to be involved in this project, even just a little bit.

I couldn't wait to spend more time with her.

Bethel

"So, where's this friend of yours?" Coach Roth asked me in his growly voice as he watched the football team run drills on the field in front of us.

I was wondering the same thing. "She'll be here soon," I said, checking my watch for the fifth time in five minutes. Jessica was supposed to go right over to Lila's, pick up the camera, and come right back. We both knew it was going to take her a while, but we'd figured out she could get back to the school before football practice was over. Now it was almost five o'clock, and the guys were going to be hitting the showers any minute. And that was something I was sure we couldn't use as part of our documentary.

"I hope nothing happened to her," I muttered. Sometimes, when Jessica was distracted, she rode her bike like a maniac. Kind of the way my dad drove his car when he was trying to get home before a Lakers game started.

"That her?" Coach Roth said, squinting across the field. "I can't see that far." I followed his gaze, and sure enough, Jessica was jogging along the edge of the field, camera in one hand, some kind of shopping bag in the other. I breathed a sigh of relief.

"Hey!" Jessica said as she approached us. "I'm so sorry I'm late." She was catching her breath as she took off her backpack and put down the shopping bag. She popped open the viewer on the camera and hit a few buttons. "Lila and I were talking, and I just lost track of time."

Coach Roth blew his whistle. "All right, boys, let's see some hustle!" he yelled. "You're being taped for posterity, so for God's sake, try not to embarrass me!"

Jessica started filming the practice, and I had to bite my lip to keep from saying what I wanted to say. She was late because she was gabbing with *Lila?* She left me here chatting with a man whose only coherent thoughts were about special teams and third-down conversions so she could dish the dirt with that girl? I couldn't help feeling a little let down by this news.

"This is great stuff!" Jessica said, following the running back as he flew by with the ball. I took a deep breath. At least we were getting started on our project. We had the camera, and now

Lila's role in this whole thing was done.

"Do you girls want a quick interview with Tommy?" Coach asked us. Tommy Villavacencia was the quarterback and captain of the team . . . and I'd had an unspoken crush on him since the second grade.

"Okay!" Jessica and I said in unison.

Coach blew his whistle again, bringing practice to an end, and summoned Tommy over. He pulled off his helmet as he trotted over to us, and I tried to remain calm. He was even cute when he was all sweaty and gross.

"What's up?" Tommy asked, eyeing us as he ran a hand through his longish, black hair.

"Can we interview you for our documentary on SVJH?" Jessica asked, keeping the camera on him.

Tommy flashed his gorgeous smile. "Sure."

Coach Roth told Tommy he'd see him in the gym and went back to the school with the rest of the team.

"So, what do you want to know?" Tommy asked. My mind went blank, and I looked at Jessica.

"Hey, I'm filming," she said. "You ask the questions."

Tommy was looking at me, smiling expectantly, so I blurted out the first thing that came to mind. "What exactly does the quarterback do?"

He laughed, Jessica looked at me with her free eye as if I had totally lost it, and I immediately wanted to smack myself. I knew what a quarterback did. I watched the Chargers games with my father every single weekend. And now Tommy V. was laughing at me.

"She means, because some of our viewers might not know," Jessica covered. I wanted to kiss her, I was so grateful.

"Okay," Tommy said, turning to the camera. "The quarterback is like the team commander . . . ," he began. As he talked, I started thinking about what my next, nonidiotic question should be and made a mental note to thank Jessica later.

"So, what's in the bag?" I asked Jessica as we walked to our bikes after leaving Tommy back at the gym. She was swinging the little purple sack back and forth so widely, I was sure she wanted me to notice and ask about it.

"Lila lent me this new shirt!" Jessica said excitedly. "Wait until you see it! Lacey's going to be so jealous. Wanna see?" She reached into the bag.

"That's okay," I said, my stomach turning slightly. She was borrowing clothes from Lila now? "I'll just wait until you wear it."

" 'Kay," Jessica said. She sounded slightly disappointed, and I felt bad, but taking it back now would be awkward. "Good job with the interview," Jessica added.

"Yeah, right," I said, rolling my eyes as we reached the bike racks. "Katie Couric, beware."

"It wasn't that bad," Jessica said. She put the camera in her backpack and pulled her arms through the straps.

"Well, thanks for saving me," I said, kneeling to unlock my bike. "I owe you one."

"Really?" Jessica said. She was fiddling with the handle on her shopping bag. "Because I kind of have a favor to ask."

Uh-oh. This didn't sound good. I snapped open my lock, pulled out the chain, and stood up. "Okay . . . ," I prompted.

"Lila wants to be in the documentary," Jessica said, unable to look me directly in the eye. "And I told her she could."

"You're kidding me," I said, annoyed. I'd thought we made an agreement. Lila was supposed to lend us the camera, and that was it. Had Jessica forgotten about that after spending one afternoon with the girl? "Why would you want to let her get involved?" I asked.

"She's not as bad as you think she is," Jessica said dismissively.

Right. Lend someone a shirt and suddenly all past wrongs are forgiven. "Are you forgetting the way she treated everyone at your party at the beginning of the year?" I asked, pulling my bike out of the rack with a clang. "She wasn't even interested in being nice to your new friends. She wasn't even interested in *meeting* us."

Jessica shrugged. "Maybe she was just intimidated or something," she said. "She didn't know anyone."

That was the point. She hadn't *wanted* to know anyone.

"C'mon," Jessica said. "Give her a chance. She'll only be in the movie a little. I will not let her take over, I swear." Jessica hung her little shopping bag off her handlebars and swung her leg over her bike. "Besides, it *is* her camera," she said, settling into her seat.

I sighed. There was no arguing with that point. And Jessica definitely wasn't going to back down. Lila was obviously important to her. Though I had no idea why. "Okay," I said finally.

Jessica grinned and let out a little squeal. "This is going to be so cool. I know you'll like her when you get to know her."

I laughed but didn't say anything. I knew Jessica believed that Lila wasn't going to take over, but sometimes Jessica is a little . . . naive, I guess. She doesn't always know people as well as she thinks she does, and she makes some kinds of silly mistakes. Like the party I kept thinking about—that whole thing was a bad idea from the beginning, but Jessica had been totally sure everything was going to be fine. Until the cops showed up, that is.

But I knew she meant well, and I hoped she was right about Lila keeping her nose out of our project. I was sure she was dead wrong about one thing, though—Lila and I getting along. I did not see it happening.

Jessica

"Hey, Jessica!" Bethel said, hurrying over to my locker on Wednesday morning. "Kristin's in for this afternoon."

"Great!" I said. I put out my arms and grinned. "So, what do you think?"

"Of what?" Bethel asked, raising one eyebrow.

"Duh! The shirt!" I said, pulling off my backpack and twirling around. "Isn't it fab?"

"It's kind of Britney Spears, isn't it?" Bethel asked as she yanked her notebook out of her bag and started rooting around in there for a pen.

I shook my head and sighed. "That's the point." Bethel was a lot of great things, but she was not up on the latest fashion trends. I decided to forget about it—I was sure Kristin would appreciate my new shirt when I saw her later.

"So it's all settled," I said, popping open my locker as Bethel looked over her notes.

"Everyone's getting together at the park this afternoon to play Frisbee."

"Cool," Bethel said with a nod. She looked up from her notebook for a moment. "Do you think this is too set up, though?" she asked. "I mean, we normally don't *all* get together after school. It's more like a weekend thing."

I emptied my books into my locker, then took out just the ones I'd need for the morning. "I know," I said. "But I want to get as much done this week as possible so we have time free if other stuff comes up and we can start editing and doing voice-overs this weekend. I think it's okay."

"Yeah, you're probably right," Bethel said, taking the camera out of my bag and looking it over. "You have to show me how to work this thing."

"Oh, it's easy," I said. "All you have to do is open the viewer and hit the green button." I pulled my hair back from my face and checked my reflection in my locker mirror. "Oh! Remind me to call Lila on her cell at lunch and tell her where to meet us," I said. I saw Bethel's face fall in the reflection and turned to face her.

"Bethel," I said. "I thought you were cool with Lila being in this."

"I am," Bethel said, avoiding my eyes. "But it's

not like she would ever come to the park to play Frisbee with Liz and Sal and Damon and everyone. Her being there will make it more like fiction than a documentary."

I took a deep breath. The girl did have a point. I wasn't sure if Lila had ever played Frisbee in her life. And I knew she'd never hung out with me and my new friends. But I really wanted her to meet them and get to know them. It would be so cool if everyone got along. Plus I wanted her to meet Damon so I could see her drool.

"You're right—she wouldn't," I said, pulling my fingers through my hair. "But we just decided that a little fudging was okay."

Bethel rolled her eyes, and I laughed, reaching over to open the viewer on the camera she still held in her hands. "C'mon," I said. "Get some exciting footage of me at my locker." I pursed my lips and struck a pose. Bethel finally caved, laughing at me. She hit the green button and pointed the camera at me just as Damon came up behind me and put his arms around my waist.

"Hey!" I said, looking up at him. "Are you coming to the park today?"

"If you're there, I'm there," Damon said, playfully kissing me on the cheek.

I blushed and held my hand up in front of the camera so Bethel couldn't see us. Then Damon and I made loud, smacking kissy noises, and Bethel filmed until we were all laughing too hard to keep it going.

That clip was definitely going to make the final cut.

Bethel

"Over here! Over here!" Salvador del Valle yelled, waving his hands in the air like a maniac as Anna Wang passed the Frisbee to her boyfriend, Toby Martin. "Oh, come on!" Salvador yelled. "How am I going to get camera time if no one will pass me the Frisbee?"

I pulled the camera away from my face. "Trust me," I said. "You're getting camera time."

"Yeah?" Salvador asked, his eyes lighting up. "Make sure you get my best side!"

I laughed and continued filming as Jessica, Elizabeth, Damon, Larissa Harris, Kristin Seltzer, Brian Rainey, Blue Spiccoli, and the others continued to play. Everyone except Salvador was acting totally normal—just as if the camera wasn't there. I was having a great time. These scenes were definitely going to make a great addition to the documentary.

"Um . . . Bethel . . . right?" someone said just behind my left shoulder. I glanced over to see Lila Fowler standing there in a lavender-and-white flowered sundress with her hair curled and her mascara applied perfectly. I looked down and saw that she was wearing strappy lavender sandals and her toenails were painted.

"Hi," I said, trying to sound friendly. "Are you going to play Frisbee in that?"

"Well, when Jessica said you were playing Frisbee, I didn't actually think you were going to be playing Frisbee," she said, looking at my friends with a disappointed expression.

I hit the off button on the camera.

"What did you think we'd be doing?" I asked, confused. Did she think Jessica was speaking in code when she invited her?

Lila let out a little laugh as Salvador dove for the Frisbee, missed, and landed on his face. "I don't know," she said. "Something a little less . . . kindergarten?"

"I'm okay! I'm all right!" Salvador said, jumping up and raising his hands in the air to show us he was still intact. He did have a huge grass stain down the front of his shirt, though.

"What's *his* deal?" Lila asked as she eyed Salvador warily.

I took a deep breath to keep myself from biting her head off. This was Jessica's friend, and even if she was never nice to me, I wasn't going to stoop to her level. "Why don't you get in the game?" I said. "You might have fun."

Lila put down her purse and walked out onto the field, where Jessica greeted her and started introducing her around. After they said hello, Blue and Salvador came jogging over to me and told me to turn on the camera again. Once it was trained on them, they started to perform.

"Now, the secret to good Frisbee is all in the wrist," Blue said quite seriously, as if he was reporting from the Olympics. He took Salvador's hand and demonstrated a weak wrist position and a strong one. "Now, Sal, here, he has a weak wrist," Blue said, slinging his arm over Salvador's shoulders.

"Hey!" Salvador said. "I do not!"

Blue grinned at the camera. "Amateurs," he said, pushing his floppy blond hair away from his forehead. "We'll turn him into a professional yet." He gave Salvador a first-class noogie, and Salvador chased him across the field, yelling the whole way.

As I panned away from them, I caught Jessica tossing the Frisbee to Lila, who raised her hands as if she was blocking it from hitting her instead of trying to catch it.

"Ow!" she squeaked. The Frisbee hit the ground, and she stared down at her hand. "Great! My nail broke!"

"Lila! I'm sorry!" Jessica said, watching as Lila stalked off the field, holding her wrist as if she had terminally injured her hand.

"I can't believe this," she muttered as I followed her with the camera. (I thought a little drama would be good for the documentary.) She saw me filming her and forced a smile, but kept walking.

I rolled my eyes and hit the off button on the camera. "Jess! It's your turn to film!" I called out. Yes, I was here to do my project, but I also wanted to have a good time. And there was no way I was going to be able to do that while standing on the sidelines with the princess.

Jessica

"So, Lila," I said, filming her as she sat on a wooden bench next to the field, filing her broken nail. "Having fun?"

"Yeah," Lila said without looking up. "Best time of my life." Then she glanced over at me, and we both laughed. I was one of the few people in the world who could tell when Lila was actually angry and when she was just *acting* sarcastic. It was a fine line.

"Omigod! What a move! I am the king!" Salvador yelled. I turned with the camera just in time to see him skidding to a stop in front of me.

"Did you get that?" he said excitedly as I struggled to refocus the camera so that his rugby shirt wasn't taking up the whole shot. "Did you catch that move?"

"Sorry," I said with a shrug. "I guess I missed it."

Salvador's black eyes widened, and he brought his hands to his forehead, clocking himself on the nose with the Frisbee.

"You missed it?" he wailed. "I caught this

thing between my legs!" Then he threw his hands in the air and loped back to the field, where everyone was standing around, waiting for him (and the Frisbee) to return. "I guess I'll just have to re-create greatness!" he shouted, causing everyone to laugh.

He tossed the Frisbee to Damon and told him to throw it back. I dutifully held up the camera, ready to catch "greatness" on film. Damon threw the Frisbee, and Salvador tried to catch it between his legs, but it bounced off his shin and landed ten feet away. He ran to get it and tossed it to Damon again, but this time when Damon threw it, it went behind Salvador and he fell on his butt trying to get it. Everyone was laughing, including Salvador. He either didn't care that everyone thought he was a goof or loved the attention.

"Okay, you're fired," he told Damon, throwing the Frisbee to Brian. "C'mon, Rainey, don't let me down," he said, bending at the knees and putting one hand behind him. Brian threw the Frisbee, and it skimmed Salvador's head.

"Ugh! What is *with* you people?" Salvador shouted, balling his fists in frustration.

I laughed and turned off the camera. We were running out of batteries, and I had a feeling Salvador wasn't going to be doing his move again anytime soon.

Jessica

"That kid is such a dork," Lila said, laughing under her breath as she tossed her nail file back into her purse and snapped it closed.

"No, he's not," I said automatically. "He's funny."

Lila raised one eyebrow. "Yeah, in a totally dorky way."

"C'mon, Li," I said, laying the camera aside. "Sal's really nice. And he's one of Liz's best friends. I used to think he was geeky too, but he's actually . . . fun." I furrowed my brow, looking out at my friends on the field. Part of me couldn't believe how easily I was defending Salvador. He *had* always kind of gotten on my nerves. But lately that had changed. I kind of liked having the big doofball around.

"Since when did you become champion of the geeks?" Lila asked, leaning back on the bench and folding her arms in front of her chest.

I swallowed hard and laughed it off. That wasn't the kind of question anyone expected you to answer, but it made me kind of uncomfortable. I didn't want to say anything to Lila and get myself on her bad side, so I just returned my attention to the Frisbee game and tried not to think about what she'd said.

Bethel

"I'm exhausted!" I said as I sat down next to Kristin after the Frisbee had finally stopped flying. Everyone was sprawled out on the grass, resting and reliving choice moments from the game.

"I'm with you, Bethel," Damon, said, slinging his arm over his eyes. "This documentary is going to kill us all!" There were a few laughs as Jessica nudged his side.

"Let's make a pact," Larissa piped in. "No more forced athleticism for the sake of stardom."

Everyone agreed, but then Blue sat up, leaning back on his elbows. "You think this was bad, you should have been there for the first day of surfing camp." He shook his head. "*That* was brutal. We were in the water for eight hours straight, and by the time they called us in to feed us, this one kid was so cold, the skin on his toes was all purple and they had to—"

"You know, you guys should try to get some other people in your documentary," Lila said suddenly, completely interrupting Blue in the middle of his story.

Blue fell silent, and we all looked at her, but she just kept talking as if she hadn't done anything blatantly rude.

"I mean, if it's all just people from SVJH, then you're not really representing Sweet Valley as a whole," she said, tearing up some grass and then letting it sprinkle out of her fingers. "It's too bad we didn't do this last year," she said, looking up at Jessica with a grin. "Imagine if we'd videotaped some of the stuff the Unicorns did? That would have been so cool. Remember when Mandy was working at the country club and we . . ."

As Lila talked, I looked around the group, and everyone was either staring at each other uncomfortably or starting their own quiet conversations. I didn't blame them. Who wanted to hear about last year and the silly club Jessica and her friends had made up? Even Jessica was usually too embarrassed about her little Unicorn club to talk about it.

Even Damon rolled over onto his side so he could talk to Brian. But Jessica looked like she was supercharged. "Yes! And then she was hiding under the table, and everyone thought she was some kind of princess or something!" she exclaimed, giggling along with Lila.

I sighed and lay down on the grass, trying to block Jessica and Lila out. Didn't Jessica see how self-absorbed the two of them were being? Part of me just wanted to say something right then and there. I mean, Jessica wasn't acting like Jessica. She was acting like a little Lila clone. But I bit my tongue and kept it to myself. This would all be over in a few days, and everything would go back to normal.

Hopefully.

Elizabeth

"Sal, are you really going to eat all of that?" I asked as I sat down at a table at Scoops with him, Anna, Larissa, Toby, and Blue. Salvador had ordered a Colossal Sundae, which consisted of six scoops of ice cream and every topping known to man. It looked big enough for all of us.

"I'm hungry after that workout," he said, rubbing his stomach. He scooped out a spoonful of ice cream that was so big, I thought it would never fit in his mouth—but it did—somehow.

"Okay," I said, taking a lick of my coffee-chip cone. "It's your digestive system." Everyone else's parents had picked them up after our game, and Jessica had gone over to Damon's to say hi to his mom and sisters. The rest of us had decided to ruin our dinners and pig out.

"I'm sorry, but didn't you think it was a little weird for that Lila girl to wear a dress to play Frisbee?" Anna asked, dipping her spoon into

Toby's sundae and coming out with a heaping spoonful of chocolate ice cream. Toby smiled, shook his head, and took some of Anna's ice cream.

"I get the feeling she would wear a dress even if she were going to dig a ditch," Salvador said, his lips covered in chocolate sauce.

"There's an image," I said, wiping my mouth. "I don't think Lila knows what a shovel is."

"Is she always like that, or was she just in a mood?" Larissa asked in a lowered voice as she leaned her elbows on the table.

I sighed and stared at my melting ice cream. "Unfortunately, she's pretty much always like that," I said.

"That's too bad," Blue lamented as he spun his straw around in his cookies-and-cream shake. "That's a sorry existence."

For a moment we all sat there in silence. Blue was right. Lila must not be all that happy if she felt the need to be so negative all the time.

"She's not that bad," I said finally, but I didn't sound very convincing. The others moved on to a conversation about their own time-capsule projects, but my mind started to wander. Even for Lila, something was off. Why was she so interested in Jessica again? Did she really just want to get her face in front of the camera?

Elizabeth

Something told me it was more than that. If I knew Lila, she wanted something else out of this whole situation.

The girl always wanted something else.

Maybe I should never have suggested that Jessica borrow Lila's camera.

"Hey! There's my brother," Blue said suddenly. I looked up to see Blue's older brother, Leaf, pulling up outside in his Range Rover. He was going to drive us all home. I slid out of the booth and grabbed a few napkins as everyone else scrambled up, gathering their things.

On our way to the door I suddenly heard a lot of giggling and looked toward the back of the room to see all of Lila's girlfriends from SVMS, hanging out at a corner table, sharing a Colossal. At least, I could have sworn it was the Double E's. That was weird. I knew Lila well enough to know that there was no way she would have missed a social gathering with her friends to hang out with *us*—random SVJH people.

"What's the matter, Liz—you get brain freeze from the ice cream?" Salvador asked, holding the door open for me with one hand while balancing his sundae cup in the other. Everyone else was already climbing into the car.

"Oh . . . sorry," I said as I walked past him. "Thanks."

As we drove off, everyone started talking about the Frisbee game again, but I couldn't stop thinking about Lila and the Double E's and wondering how Jessica fit in. What was going on?

Bethel

"Okay, that was icky," Jessica said as she slid into a chair in the cafeteria on Thursday afternoon and pulled out a brown-bagged lunch from her backpack. "I am so glad my mom made me tuna this morning."

I looked down at my own tray of meatballs and fries and swallowed hard. We'd just finished filming the behind-the-counter footage of the cafeteria kitchen—at Jessica's insistence. There wasn't anything horrible back there—no bugs or mice or whatever—but it wasn't quite as *clean* as I would have liked it to be. And the big vats of food weren't too appealing either. I know they have to cook for hundreds of kids, but I never needed to know how it was accomplished.

"So, what do you want to film after school today?" I asked, pushing back my tray. I needed to give it a few minutes before I dug in. "I checked to see which clubs were having meetings, and we could go to the environmental club, the literary-magazine meeting, or the astronomy club."

Jessica slowly chewed a bite of her sandwich. "I don't know," she said. "None of those would exactly make for exciting footage. . . ."

"How about following the janitor around as he cleans?" I said, my eyes lighting up. "I bet he finds some sick stuff!"

"Um . . . Bethel?" Jessica said, putting down her bottle of water. For the first time I noticed she was looking a bit pale.

My stomach turned. I had a feeling I was not going to like what was coming. "What?" I asked.

"I kinda told Lila we'd go to the mall this afternoon and I'd film us shopping," Jessica said.

My mouth actually dropped open like something out of a cartoon. She'd already planned this afternoon, and I was just hearing about it *now?* "Jessica, you can't make decisions like that without telling me," I said, leaning back in my chair and gripping the sides of the seat. "Weren't we supposed to be working on this project together?"

"I know, I'm sorry," Jessica said. She pushed her hair behind her ears and slumped a little. "But I really think we *should* film the mall. It's a huge part of the Sweet Valley social scene."

"I know, but—"

"You can totally come with us," Jessica interrupted. "I just figured shopping wasn't exactly your thing."

I took a deep breath, staring at my cooling food as I tried to calm myself down. "Fine," I said. "I don't care. Just next time, tell me before you decide to do something like this."

"Okay," Jessica said, picking up her sandwich again as if nothing had happened. "I swear I'll get some really great stuff. You'll love it!"

I picked up my plastic fork and started poking at the meatballs on my plate. I don't think I could have possibly been more annoyed. Jessica had promised Lila wouldn't get too involved in our project, but now I felt like the girl was totally taking over.

Elizabeth

The doorbell rang on Thursday afternoon, and I opened the door to find Lila standing there, wearing sunglasses that practically swallowed her whole face. Obviously they were the latest fashion.

"Hello, Liz!" she said in an enthusiastic, singsongy voice—as if we hadn't just seen each other the day before.

"Hi, Lila," I said, stepping aside so she could come in.

"I'll be right down!" Jessica yelled from her room upstairs.

"Okay!" I yelled back.

I closed the door, and Lila and I just stood there in the entryway for a moment, saying nothing and looking around like we'd never seen an entryway before. We never had had much to talk about.

"So . . . what's up?" I said, feeling awkward in the silence.

"Not much," Lila answered. "We're going shopping."

Elizabeth

There was a shocker. Part of me really wanted to ask about the Double E's and why she wasn't with them the day before. I'd been wondering about it on and off all day—whenever I'd let my mind wander in class. But I knew it would sound suspect coming from me. I decided to try to be vague.

"How's school?" I asked, leaning back against the doorway that led to the living room. "How are your friends?"

"The Double E's? They're fine," Lila said with a wave of her hand. Her voice was a little strained, though, and she started examining her split ends. Although from what I could see she didn't have any.

"You should have brought them to the park yesterday," I said. I felt a little bit bad about prodding, but I really wanted to know if the girl was up to something—for Jessica's sake. "I'm sure they would have had fun."

"Oh, they definitely would have come, but we had a marathon Boosters practice yesterday. They were at school until, like, six o'clock," Lila said, never once looking me in the eye. "I ditched it for Jessica, but we couldn't *all* not show up for practice."

"Right," I said, looking down at my feet. I felt my face flush because I knew she was lying.

When I'd seen her friends at Scoops, it was a little before five o'clock. And they hadn't even been wearing Boosters uniforms or workout clothes. Besides, Lila's face was all red, just like it always was when she lied.

She must be fighting with her friends or something. Which meant she was probably using Jessica because she had no one else to hang out with. It all made sense. Lila had shown zero interest in Jessica since we transferred to SVJH, and now they'd hung out almost every day this week. I wanted to say something, but I had no idea what it would be, and I didn't have time to decide. Jessica came bounding down the stairs with Lila's camera, decked out for an afternoon at the mall.

"Ready?" Lila asked, opening the door. She looked and sounded relieved.

"Valley Mall, beware!" Jessica answered with a grin.

I watched through the window as they walked over to Lila's waiting limo and climbed inside, gabbing all the way. It sure looked like nothing had changed between them. I hoped I was wrong about Lila. She'd ditched Jessica before, and Jessica had been devastated. I didn't want to see it happen again.

Jessica

"We have to go in here!" Lila said, rushing into BCBG. "Daddy's taking me to Rome in a couple of weeks, and I have to have a new coat."

I followed Lila into the store, the camera bumping around as I rushed along to keep up with her. I'd never realized how tough it could be to navigate a mall with a practically professional shopper while having a camera permanently attached to my eye.

"We've gone on the best vacations this year," Lila said as she tore through a rack of clothes. "I've already been to New York for three weekends, we went to Paris for two weeks this summer, and over Columbus Day we went to San Francisco. I love traveling."

I didn't say anything because I didn't really have much to add to the conversation. Unless she wanted to hear about the camping trip my family had taken in August, but I had a feeling Lila wouldn't be interested in the new tent my dad had bought for me and Elizabeth.

"But enough about me," Lila said, apparently finding nothing she wanted since she was on her way out again. "What's up with you? Like, are those people I met yesterday really your friends?"

"Um . . . yeah," I said, trying to follow her along the concourse and wondering why she was asking that question in that disbelieving tone of voice.

"Really?" she asked, raising her eyebrows at the camera as she walked. "Even that Salvador person?"

I was starting to sweat, both from the exertion of keeping up with Lila and from the direction the conversation was taking. Were we really going to go through this whole thing again?

"Yes," I said with a sigh. "Sal is my friend; he's Liz's friend. We like him, okay?"

"Okay!" Lila said, laughing and throwing up her hands. "But that girl . . . what's her name? Beth? Bethany?"

"Bethel," I said, swallowing hard. I tripped over my own feet and wished there were a way to see through the camera and watch the ground at the same time.

Jessica

"Bethel, right. What a horrible name," Lila said, stopping to look in the window at The Limited. "And she's so rude. You're just hanging out with her because you got paired up for this project, right?"

My heart squeezed, and I had to grip the camera tightly to keep it from sliding out of my hand. "Bethel? No . . . I—"

"I mean, she's such a dork," Lila said, cutting me off. She was studying an outfit one of the mannequins was wearing and didn't even seem to realize how mean she was being. "We should have brought her with us today. Maybe we could have made her buy an outfit that didn't look like it was fished out of the trash."

"Whatever," I muttered, wiping my brow. Lila has always cared a lot about what other people wear. And I knew if I argued with her over it now, we'd get into a thirty-minute-long conversation about the importance of appearance.

"You should ditch her, Jess," Lila said. She lifted her eyes and stared directly at the camera as if she was trying to make a serious point. "She's a charity case. You could do so much better."

I swallowed hard and took the camera away

from my face. I had to change the subject before I self-destructed or started an argument. "Can we go get something to drink?" I asked. "I'm dying."

"Oh! Look at you!" Lila said, coming over and grabbing my wrists. "You're all red. Why don't we turn off the camera and go to the food court?"

"Sounds like a plan," I said, hitting the off button as I made a mental note to erase that footage later. It wasn't exactly something I wanted Bethel to see, or anyone else, for that matter.

"You know what we should do?" Lila said as we headed off down the hall. "We should go to that new makeup store and get makeovers. Daddy gave me a note that says I can use his credit card, so I can buy us both a few things."

"Cool!" I said, smiling. I missed doing makeovers and girlie stuff like that with Lila. Elizabeth wasn't into that stuff, and Bethel would rather be caught dead than at a makeup counter. "All the colors I have now are so boring."

"Please," Lila said, hooking her arm around mine. "You always look good, Wakefield."

I laughed and shook my head. "Thanks," I said. "You're a liar, but thanks."

Jessica

We got to the food court and walked right up to the salad bar, just like we always used to. As we waited in line, I couldn't stop smiling. Lila might not be very accepting of other people, but she'd always been a good friend to me, and I loved hanging out with her. I really did.

Lila

I looked at my reflection in the dressing-room mirror, straightened the black skirt I was wearing, and smiled. This outfit was way sophisticated. I might just have to make use of Daddy's credit card on this one.

"I'm coming out!" I yelled.

"Camera's ready!" Jessica said.

I flung aside the curtain that divided the dressing room from the rest of the store and pursed my lips, hamming it up like a model.

"Give me love, give me love," Jessica joked, panning around me with the camera.

I was about to do a little catwalk when I heard a familiar voice across the room. I looked over to see Ashlee, Courtnee, and Maree walking into the store, talking, laughing, and carrying so many bags, they had to have been at the mall all afternoon.

And once again I hadn't been informed about it.

My heart fell. For a second I wanted to jump back into the dressing room and hide until they left, but then I got ahold of myself. It wasn't like *I'd* done anything wrong. And besides, now was the perfect time to tell them all about the documentary.

"Hi, guys!" I shouted, waving them over.

"Hey, Lila!" Maree said, leading the way across the store. When the three of them reached the dressing rooms, I watched in satisfaction as they took in my killer outfit, then looked at Jessica and noticed the camera. They were obviously intrigued.

"What's going on?" Courtnee asked. She was trying to sound nonchalant, but I could tell by her face that she was dying to know what we were filming.

"You guys remember Jessica, right?" I said, putting my arm around Jessica's shoulders.

The four of them said hello to each other. The Double E's were still looking at the camera curiously.

"Well, Jessica's making a documentary about . . ." I quickly racked my brain. If I said she was doing a film about SVJH, that would bring up too many questions about my involvement. Plus it would make it sound like I wasn't supposed to be there.

"About me and my life in Sweet Valley," I said finally, grinning from ear to ear.

Jessica shot me a look, but I shot her one right back, and I knew she wouldn't say anything. It didn't really matter what the Double E's thought her movie was about.

"Wow! Really?" Maree said, her eyes shining. "What's it for?"

"It's probably going to be on TV," I said, flipping my hair over my shoulder.

"You're kidding!" Courtnee said. "That's so cool."

"Yeah, why didn't you tell us about this before?" Ashlee asked.

I cleared my throat and fiddled with the tag hanging from my sleeve. "Well, we just started," I said. "Right, Jess?"

"Yeah!" she said, kind of loudly. "Just this week, actually."

Ashlee looked from Jessica to me and back again. I couldn't figure out what she was thinking, but she looked a little skeptical. "Well, we'll let you get back to work, then," she said. "My mom's picking us up soon anyway."

I smiled as they walked away. That went pretty well. As long as they were going to keep dissing me, I might as well let them know that I had better things to do.

Unfortunately, that didn't make me feel better about the fact that they had made plans without me . . . again.

Jessica's Journal

I had such a good time with Lila yesterday. And she bought me a whole bag full of makeup. I tried to tell her she didn't have to, but . . . well, I didn't really try <u>that</u> hard.

It was kind of uncomfortable when we bumped into her friends, though. I didn't know what to say when she lied to them. I hoped they bought it when I backed her up. It's no big deal. I mean, that's just good old Lila showing off. She has this way of exaggerating, and you have to get used to taking everything she says with a grain of salt.

And she did kind of rag on my friends. I mean, fine, I understand that when you first meet Salvador, he comes off as seriously dorky. But some of that stuff she said about Bethel was totally uncalled for. I guess Lila just doesn't realize how close I am with Bethel. She never would have said that stuff if she knew.

Jessica

Friday morning on my way into school, I realized I'd forgotten to take the mall footage out of the camera. I went directly to my locker, popped out the tape, and replaced it with a blank one, putting the Lila tape in the bottom of my locker. I'd bring it home after school and erase the whole Sal-Bethel conversation.

"Hey!" Damon said, coming up behind me. I jumped at the sound of his voice. I was so deep in concentration, he'd scared me.

"You okay?" Damon asked as I turned around to face him and looked up into his perfect blue eyes. "You look . . . not okay."

"I'm fine," I said, giving him a good-morning hug.

"How did yesterday's filming at the mall go?" he asked, pulling away.

"Okay," I said quickly, not really wanting to talk about it. "I didn't get that much, actually." At least there wouldn't be that much left when I was done erasing all the stuff I had to erase.

"Oh yeah?" Damon asked, with a lopsided smile. "I thought you said Lila could shop for hours."

"She did," I answered with a laugh as I stuffed some books into my bag. "It just wasn't all camera worthy." *If Lila ever heard me say that, she'd kill me,* I thought, slamming my locker door.

"Well," Damon said, hooking his arm around my shoulders. "I was going to tell you that you should come film our lit-magazine meeting next week, but we're going to be selecting the final pieces for the issue, and that's top secret."

"What? You're not going to give your girlfriend the scoop?" I asked, faking disbelief.

"Some things are more important than a scoop, Jess," he said, faking seriousness right back.

"We'll see about that," I said. I took his hand and laced my fingers through his, already forgetting what was bothering me.

As we walked to class, I couldn't stop thinking about how glad I was to have Damon as a boyfriend . . . and how cool our lives were at that very moment. I wouldn't have traded him, or any of my friends, for the world. . . .

Bethel

When the bell rang after history class on Friday, I gathered up my stuff and looked at Jessica out of the corner of my eye. I hadn't spoken to her yet that day, and I was wondering how the mall thing had gone the day before. She looked at me and smiled, and we made our way to the front of the room together.

"I tried to call you last night, but your dad said you weren't home yet," I said, pulling my bag up onto my shoulders.

"Yeah, we were at the mall really late," Jessica said. "I was going to call you when I got home, but I had to do my homework, and when I was done, it was already after ten o'clock."

"That's okay," I said flatly. We walked in silence for a second, which was weird for us. I had this great idea for something we could film over the weekend, but I realized I was actually nervous to ask her about it. If she told me Lila was having a pool party she just *had* to film, I might lose it right there in the hallway.

"So," I said finally, averting my eyes. "My family is throwing this huge barbecue for my aunt's birthday this weekend, and I thought it might be cool to film—you know—for the family angle," I added. "The whole extended family will be there, grandparents, cousins, babies, the whole deal." I looked at her and rolled back my shoulders, ready to defend my position.

"That sounds great!" she said, completely sincere. "When is it?"

"Sunday afternoon," I answered, surprised at how psyched she sounded. I'd been so sure she was going to reject it.

"I have to clear it with my mom, but if she says it's okay, I'm totally there," Jessica said. "It's a really good idea."

"Cool," I said, smiling. We came to the end of the hall, where we had to split so I could go to English and she could go to math. "I'll see you later," I said.

"Later!" Jessica answered before speeding off.

As soon as she was gone, I let out a sigh of relief. That had gone better than I'd thought it would. At least Lila hadn't totally brainwashed her.

Jessica

On Sunday afternoon I headed over to Bethel's house on my bike. When I turned onto her street, there was a line of cars parked out in front of her house that took up the whole block, and I could hear the noise coming from her backyard. I smiled and pedaled a little harder.

After leaning my bike up against the garage, I walked around back and saw the total craziness that was going on. There were four picnic tables covered by colorful tablecloths that fluttered in the breeze. Tons of food were laid out buffet style, and people were sitting in chairs under the trees at the side of the yard, getting some shade.

"Hello, Jessica!" Bethel's mother called out to me as she poured a glass of lemonade for an older lady who was settling into a lawn chair. "Can I get you anything?"

"Hi, Mrs. McCoy. I'm not hungry yet, thanks." I put down my backpack and took out the camera. "Is Bethel around?"

"How could you miss her?" she said with a

laugh, motioning toward the other side of the yard. At that moment I heard a loud shriek and saw Bethel running around with about seven little kids, all of whom were screaming and laughing.

"Good point," I said. I turned on the camera and started filming their game of tag before Bethel and her cousins even noticed I was there. This was too cute to miss.

"You're it!" Bethel exclaimed when she caught a little girl whose hair was pulled back into three ponytails. The girl laughed and took off after the rest of the crowd of kids. Bethel took a deep breath, looked up, and spotted me. "Hey! Jess!" she said with a wave.

I clicked off the camera and wove through the crowd to join her. "Are you out of breath?" I asked, surprised. I'd hardly ever seen Bethel stop for air—even after running a four-hundred-meter dash.

"I've been playing tag for like ten hours," she said, fanning herself with her hand. "These monsters get up at six o'clock . . . on Sunday!" She smiled and watched as they all tore by us in a line, the girl who was it bringing up the rear. "You can't not love them, though," she added.

I smiled. Who knew Bethel was a sucker for kids? "I thought you were a tough chick," I teased.

"Don't tell anyone," Bethel joked. She grabbed my arm and pulled me toward the tables. "I want to introduce you to my grandparents and the birthday girl."

A couple of hours later I was stuffed with barbecued chicken, had added a little color to my tan, and was running out of tape. Bethel was in the middle of the yard, wrestling with her cousins, but I couldn't move out of the plastic chair I'd dumped myself into after the cake had come out. I didn't know where her energy was coming from, but I was perfectly content right where I was.

Bethel broke away from the kids and walked over to me. "Wanna join us?"

"Nah," I said, patting my stomach. "I think I ate too much. Your mom can *cook*."

"Yeah, she knows," Bethel said with a laugh.

"I'd better get going." I told her, pushing myself out of my chair. "I actually have a little bit of nonhistory homework to do."

"Okay," Bethel said with a grin. "Did we get good stuff?" she asked, motioning to the camera.

"Are you kidding?" I exclaimed. "This party was great. And that story your grandmother told about how you refused to wear diapers was classic."

Jessica

"Okay, that's not going in the documentary," Bethel said, leveling me with a glare.

I laughed. "Maybe it will, maybe it won't." I tucked the camera into my backpack and tugged on the shoulder straps. "Seriously, though. I had an awesome time," I told her.

"Cool," Bethel said. I could tell she was kind of proud of her family and glad I had enjoyed myself with them. As I said good-bye to her parents and made my way back to my bike, I couldn't stop smiling. I was glad Bethel had invited me and introduced me to all those people that meant so much to her—documentary or not.

Lila

Sunday evening I was sitting in my room, watching a movie on my DVD player and trying not to look at the phone. But every once in a while my eyes would wander over and I would find myself just staring at it, willing it to ring. I mean, I couldn't believe it. I hadn't spoken to my friends all weekend. Not one of them. Not once. This was unacceptable.

I sighed and clicked off the television, staring up at my canopy. How had this happened? We'd spent all of Friday just making small talk, and at the end of the day I'd been almost scared to ask them what they wanted to do this weekend—just in case they already had plans and didn't want to include me. Apparently that had been the case because here it was, eighteen-fifteen on Sunday night, and I hadn't heard from them. I wondered what they'd done all weekend.

"Ugh!" I groaned, pulling a pillow over my face. I felt so pathetic—waiting to be invited to something. That never happened to me. Usually

I was the one setting up the social calendar. I couldn't take this feeling. And I didn't know what to do about it. How was I supposed to know? Nothing even remotely like this had ever happened to me before.

I pulled away the pillow and looked at the phone again. Of course, it wasn't ringing.

"Okay! That's it!" I said to the empty room. I shoved myself off the bed, grabbed the phone, and stalked over to my closet. Then I tossed the whole thing onto the closet floor and slammed the door.

"Out of sight, out of mind," I muttered, returning to my bed. That was what my dad always said when he hid the junk food he wasn't supposed to eat.

I just hoped he was right.

Jessica

Monday after the last bell rang, I slowly made my way to my locker. Something was bugging me. All day I'd felt like I'd been forgetting something. In every class I waited for the teacher to ask for some homework assignment I hadn't done. Between classes I kept thinking someone was going to come up to me and ask me why I hadn't come to their party over the weekend. But it hadn't happened. I'd made it through the day. Still, something was nagging at the back of my head. What was I forgetting?

"Hey, Ronald," I said to my locker partner, who was already there, gathering his stuff.

"Hey!" he said with a huge smile. "How's the documentary going?"

That's when I remembered what I'd been trying to remember all day. The tape! Thank God Ronald had reminded me. I really needed to erase that mall footage before I totally forgot about it. I crouched to the floor and reached into my locker for the cassette. Then I shifted a

Jessica

few of my books around and felt around for it again. Where was it? My heart started to pound. I pulled everything out of the bottom of the locker—gym clothes, notebooks, crushed papers. There was even an apple that looked like it had been there since the beginning of the year. But no tape.

"What's wrong?" Ronald asked as I stood up again.

I pushed my hair off my sweaty forehead. "Ronald, have you seen a videotape? I left one in our locker last week."

"Yeah, Bethel took it," he said casually. As if he hadn't just said the worst thing I could have possibly heard at that moment.

My heart hit the floor. I could hardly breathe. "What do you mean, Bethel took it?" I asked, standing up slowly.

Ronald must have picked up on how freaked out I was because it took him a second to answer. "She . . . uh . . . came by at the end of seventh period and said her study-hall teacher was going to let her go to the AV room to work on your project," Ronald said, gripping his notebook. "So I let her have the tape."

I let out a long moan and closed my eyes. I was dead.

"Was that . . . wrong?" Ronald asked.

"You know what?" I snapped, grabbing my bag. "I don't remember ever telling you it was okay to hand out my personal stuff."

"I'm sorry!" Ronald said, turning white. "I just thought—"

"Forget it!" I said. I took off for the AV room without looking back. Maybe I wasn't too late. Maybe Bethel had spent eighth period going over our other tapes and hadn't even gotten to the shopping segment yet.

"Please, please, please don't let her be watching it," I muttered, dodging all the kids who were rushing for their buses and rides.

I made it to the AV room and flung open the door. Bethel was sitting there with her back to me, watching a big TV. She didn't move a muscle when I came in. One glance at the TV told me I was too late. Lila was on the screen, walking out of the mall and heading for the limo. The shopping trip was over, which meant Bethel had seen . . .

She picked up the remote, clicked off the VCR, and slowly turned around. Her eyes were so angry and hurt, and they were glistening with tears. Just looking at her sent an awful pain into my heart. Bethel McCoy didn't cry over anything. She once told me she hadn't even cried when she broke her arm. Now she was about to break down, and it was all my fault.

Jessica

"Bethel, I—" But I couldn't think of a single thing to say. I just stood there like an idiot while she stared at me.

"You didn't even defend me," Bethel said, her voice cracking. She cleared her throat and took a deep breath. "That's what really gets to me. You didn't say one thing to defend me."

With that, she stormed by, practically shoving me out of the way since I was still standing in front of the door. The second she was gone, I burst into tears, but I didn't go after her. What could I say?

I just slumped into a chair and cried.

Bethel

On my way out of school I didn't look anyone in the eye. A couple of people said hello to me, but I just kept staring straight ahead, refusing to let the tears spill over. I'd never been so humiliated in my life. I couldn't believe the things Lila had said about me, but worse than what was said was the fact that my so-called best friend hadn't told her off. She hadn't said *anything*. I was afraid that if I looked at anyone, I was just going to burst into tears. And I never cried. I wasn't even used to this feeling.

I made it outside and took a long, deep breath of fresh air. For a split second I felt better, but then the sound of Lila's pinched voice seeped into my brain.

"Bethel, right. What a horrible name. . . . You're just hanging out with her because you got paired up for this project, right?"

And Jessica said nothing. The tears stung my eyes as I headed for the sidewalk. My sight got all blurry, and the more I blinked, the worse it got.

"I mean, she's such a dork. . . . You should ditch her, Jess. She's a charity case. You could do so much better."

And what had Jessica said? *"Whatever."* That was it. Maybe she did think she could do better.

The second I hit the sidewalk, I started jogging, and within minutes I was tearing toward home at top speed. Maybe if I ran as fast as I could, people wouldn't notice the tears streaming down my cheeks.

Jessica

"I can't believe I'm such a jerk, Liz,"
I said, blowing my nose as I lay on her bed on
Monday afternoon. I'd barely stopped crying for
five minutes since I'd seen Bethel. All I could
think about was the look on her face and the
tears in her eyes. How could I have done that to
her? I couldn't believe that I'd forgotten to erase
the tape. But even worse, I couldn't believe I'd
done anything bad enough that I'd felt the need
to erase it.

"Why am I like that when I'm around Lila?" I
asked, propping myself up on her pillows and
staring at the crumpled tissue in my hand. "I always do such stupid things."

"Jess," Elizabeth said as she sat down on the
edge of the bed. "This may sound like a weird
question, but . . . do you even like Lila?"

"Of course I do!" I said without even thinking
about it. I wiped the tears off my cheeks. "We've
been best friends since birth!"

"Yeah, but—"

"Just because we haven't been hanging out with each other lately doesn't mean I don't *like* her." I tossed my dirty tissue in the direction of Elizabeth's garbage can, and it hit the floor about a foot away. I sighed and crossed my arms over my chest. "We've always been friends."

"Okay." Elizabeth brought one leg up onto the bed and turned to face me. "But think about it for a second. I mean, *really* think about it. Over the past few days, when were you actually having fun? When were you laughing and actually enjoying yourself?"

I took a deep breath and let it out slowly, thinking over the last week. I'd had a lot of fun at Bethel's on Sunday, stuffing our faces and playing with her cousins. And I'd had a great time playing Frisbee with our friends last week. Salvador and Damon had had me doubled over, laughing so hard, I was in pain.

I'd had fun with Lila at the mall, but I'd also been really stressed. I was never sure what to say or do. The best part of the day was the makeover we'd had. And that was mostly fun because I was relieved we weren't slamming my friends anymore.

"Jessica?" Elizabeth said.

"You know what? You're right," I said, looking into Elizabeth's eyes. "All the girl talks about is clothes and makeup and the stupid Double E's! Everything is all about her!"

"Exactly," Elizabeth said.

I leaned back, my mind swimming. How could I have let a person like Lila get to me so completely that I had ruined my friendship with Bethel? What the heck was wrong with me?

About an hour later I rang the doorbell at Lila's house, fuming. Elizabeth had told me to call Lila and tell her how I felt, but all I wanted to do was return her camera and tell her right to her face that I didn't like the way she'd treated me. She'd been blatantly rude about my friends. I didn't care if my friends were cool in Lila's book. I didn't care if they were the most popular people in school. Maybe that stuff used to be important to me, but it wasn't anymore. And I had let Lila make me forget that.

All this time I'd been at SVJH, meeting new people and making new friends—making real friends who actually cared about me—and in just a couple of days Lila had turned everything around. It was really kind of amazing when you thought about it.

I said hello to Hester when she let me in and took the stairs two at a time. All I could think was that this would probably be the last time I was ever in Lila's house. And the thought didn't really bother me that much.

"Lila?" I said as I walked into her room.

She came out of her closet, holding a black dress that still had the tags on it. "Jess?" she said with a smile. "Hey! What are you doing here?" She flung the dress onto her bed and turned to face me, but the moment she really looked at me, the smile fell right off her face. "What's wrong?" she asked.

"I'll tell you what's wrong," I said, keeping my voice low but firm. I placed the camera, along with her shirt, on her bed next to her dress. She just looked at her stuff for a second as if she didn't know what it was. "I'm sick of you ragging on my friends," I fumed. "And I'm tired of hearing all about how you rule the school and all that stupid stuff."

"Jessica—"

I took a step back. "In fact, I'm tired of being your friend, period," I said, tossing my hair over my shoulder. "All you care about is yourself and what you want to do and where you want to go. You don't care about anyone else's feelings. Because of you, Bethel may never talk to me again. And she's a real friend. You are not worth it, Lila. So not worth it."

Lila's mouth was hanging open, and she

looked like I had just slapped her in the face. Actually, I kind of felt like I had. Maybe I was being a little harsh, but I was angry and hurt. Lila couldn't treat people the way she did and get away with it.

Finally she slowly closed her mouth and lifted her chin. "I want you to leave," she said. "And don't ever come back here."

"Gladly," I said. Then I turned on my heel and stalked out of the room, slamming the door behind me.

Lila

For a second after Jessica left, I just stood there in the middle of my bedroom and stared at the door she'd literally slammed in my face. How could she do that? Had she totally lost it? I couldn't believe she'd walked right into *my* house—uninvited—and yelled at me like that. Plus I didn't even know what she was talking about. What had I done to make her go postal?

I stalked over to my window and watched Jessica tear away on her bike, going so fast, she almost skidded out at the end of the driveway.

"Unreal!" I shouted at the empty room. I walked over to the bed and picked up the camera, then pulled the box it had come in out from under my bed and tossed the camera inside. This whole thing had started because she'd begged me to borrow *my* camera. How ungrateful could a person possibly be?

I was so angry, I felt like I was going to explode. When I realized I was pacing around my room with my fists clenched, I realized I had to do something to vent. I wanted to punch some-thing, but that was out of the question.

"I have to tell Ashlee about this," I muttered. Ashlee would sympathize. She would be just as indignant as I was, and that was exactly what I needed that moment—someone to tell me I was right—especially since Jessica hadn't given me a second to retaliate.

I turned around to grab my phone and noticed that the cord was lying on the floor. It crossed the room and disappeared under my closet door. At that moment it all came back to me. I couldn't call Ashlee because she basically wasn't talking to me. We hadn't said much to each other at school that day—just polite small talk. And it was the same with Maree and Courtnee. I had a sudden dread in the pit of my stomach. I didn't even have anyone I could vent to.

I sat down on the edge of my bed and took a deep breath. "I don't care about anyone else's feelings?" I muttered, remembering the awful things Jessica had said to me. If there was any-one I knew who didn't care about anyone else's feelings, it was Ashlee, Courtnee, and Maree. They'd been leaving me out of everything and acting like it didn't even matter. And now, when I really needed a friend, I knew none of them would even care. Why would they want to hear about what Jessica had done to me when they didn't even care enough to invite me to go shopping with them? It just wasn't fair.

I felt a tear roll down my cheek and wiped it away. I was not going to cry over this. I didn't need these people. But the tears kept coming, and I realized it was pointless to try to stop it. I lay back on my bed, pressed my face into my comforter, and sobbed.

Bethel

Monday night I was sitting at my desk with my history notebook open in front of me, trying to figure out what I could possibly do for the time-capsule project. What could I make that would be interesting and different . . . and that could be done by Wednesday morning?

"Thanks a lot, Jessica," I muttered, doodling an arrow in the margin of my notebook. I pressed down so hard, I broke the point of my pencil and ripped the page.

I was getting nowhere because every time I tried to concentrate, my mind flashed back on everything that had happened earlier that day. I would be on the verge of coming up with an idea when I would hear Lila's voice again, talking about how awful I was, or see myself running away from school crying like a baby, or see Jessica just standing there in the AV room, looking like she'd been caught doing something really bad.

She didn't even try to stop me and explain when I ran out. She just looked guilty. I was sure she cared more about the fact that she'd been snagged than the fact that she'd hurt my feelings—big time. My eyes were still aching and dry from being all cried out.

Suddenly the phone rang, and I practically jumped at the sound. My heart started pounding. Maybe it was Jessica calling to apologize. It was about time anyway. I took a deep breath and tried to calm myself down as I waited for someone to answer the phone.

"If it is her, I'm not even going to listen," I told myself, pretending to concentrate on my project ideas. "There's no excuse for what she did." In fact, it was after ten o'clock, and Jessica knew I wasn't supposed to get calls after ten. What was she trying to do, get me grounded on top of everything else?

"I'm definitely not going to talk to her," I said. I looked down, and my pen was poised over my notebook. I realized I was waiting for my mom to call up the stairs and tell me to pick up the phone. I was *hoping* it was Jessica. Pathetic. I was totally pathetic.

I looked at the closed door of my bedroom, then leaned back in my chair and sighed, flinging my pen down on my desk. It had been too long. The phone call obviously wasn't for me.

"It's fine," I said, slumping down farther in my chair. "I *really* didn't want to talk to her anyway."

Right. If that was true, then why was I more depressed than ever?

Jessica

"Are you sure you don't want me to come with you?" Elizabeth asked as we stopped at the corner of Bethel's street on Tuesday morning. We were on our way to school, and I'd decided to take a detour to Bethel's house to see if I could get her to talk to me.

"That's okay," I said, pushing my hair out of my face as a breeze tried to blow it all over the place. "I don't want it to seem like we're ganging up on her or whatever." Inside I was dying to have Elizabeth come with me. I was so nervous, my palms were sweating, and my heart was pounding really fast. Having Elizabeth there would have made me feel much better. But this was my problem. I had to deal with it myself.

"All right," Elizabeth said, backing up a couple of steps. "But find me before first period. I want to know what happened."

"I will," I said. I stood there for a second, clutching the strap on my backpack as I watched her cross the street and disappear around the next corner. Then I stood there a little while longer. "Okay, move," I told myself. "Get it over with."

I made myself turn around and walk the rest of the way to Bethel's house. My knees were shaking slightly as I approached her door, but I tried to give myself a pep talk. Maybe it wouldn't be so bad. Maybe she would just accept my apology and we could put all this craziness behind us.

I climbed the steps and rang the doorbell before I could chicken out and run. A moment later Bethel opened the door, shrugging into her jacket. She was obviously on her way out to school, but the second she saw me, she froze.

"What are you doing here?" she snapped, stepping out of the house and pulling the door closed behind her.

I got a chill when I heard her tone. She might as well have been talking to a gnat. "I . . . uh . . . I wanted to see if you wanted to walk to school together," I said as she brushed right past me and started down the front walk.

"Why would I want to walk to school with you?" she asked, not even looking over her shoulder.

My heart plummeted. "C'mon, Bethel," I said, jogging to catch up with her.

She looked at me out of the corner of her eye

and picked up her pace. "I guess it's a free country," she said.

Okay, so Bethel wasn't going to make this easy. I understood that. Her feelings had been majorly hurt, and it was all my fault. But I knew she would let me make it up to her. We were friends. She had to forgive me.

"Listen," I said, struggling to keep up without losing my breath. "I just wanted you to know that I talked to Lila . . . I mean, I yelled at Lila, actually," I said. I snorted a laugh, hoping she would cheer up at the news, but Bethel didn't even blink. She just kept walking and glaring straight ahead.

I cleared my throat and tried again. "I realized what a jerk she was being and what a jerk *I* was when I was hanging out with her, so I went over to her house last night and told her exactly what I thought of her."

There. Bethel had to appreciate that. The direct approach was just her style.

"Bethel?" I prompted when she didn't react.

She stopped and turned to look at me, but she was still glaring. "What do you want, a medal or something?" she snapped. "None of this changes what you did!" With that, she turned on her heel and rushed away so quickly, I couldn't have possibly caught up with her.

It didn't matter anyway because I was so shocked by her reaction, I couldn't move. I just stood there on the sidewalk with my mouth hanging open, feeling like she'd just punched me in the stomach. All I could do was watch her go.

Bethel

"So, does anyone want to give a shot at interpreting this poem?" Miss Janney asked in English class on Tuesday morning. I just ducked my head and tried to look like I was busy analyzing the poem in question—the one I hadn't read, even though it was assigned for homework last night. I started to sweat as she scanned the room, sure she was going to call on me.

"Blue?" Miss Janney said finally. I let out a sigh of relief. I was safe for now. Blue would probably give a good fifteen-minute-long explanation of how the sixteen-line poem changed his life. Not that there was anything wrong with that.

I took a deep breath and returned to the note I'd been writing before Miss Janney had asked for volunteers. So far, all it said was *Dear Jessica* on the top line of the notebook page. I wasn't even sure if *that* was right. Did I really want to call her "dear" after everything that had happened?

But I couldn't stress about little things like that. Not if I was going to get this done before the end of the class. And I wanted to get this out of the way so I could forget about the whole thing.

Dear Jessica, I wrote. *I just wanted to let you know I'm going to be working on my own project for history class.* ~~I hope~~

No. I was about to write that I hoped the documentary would come out okay, but I didn't want to hope anything for her. I was mad. I didn't care how her project went.

But even thinking that made my heart feel heavy. The documentary was supposed to be so much fun. It was an awesome idea, and we'd had such a good time messing around with our friends, interviewing teachers and custodians and coaches, getting behind-the-scenes footage. I remembered how excited I'd been about it and sighed. It was amazing how much things could change in one week.

"I'm not going to feel sorry for myself," I whispered, pushing myself up in my chair. I looked around to make sure no one had heard me, but they were all listening to Blue's explanation of the red imagery in the poem. Whatever that meant.

Jessica, I wrote, starting over. *I'm doing my own project for history. Just thought I'd let you know. And I*

think it's only fair that you *explain to Mr. Harriman.*
—Bethel.

I looked down at what I'd written, clutching my pen in one hand and the edge of the desk with the other. Was it too cold? Jessica had tried to apologize that morning—even if her apology was totally lame. She hadn't even really admitted she'd done anything wrong. She'd sort of blamed it all on Lila. Still, she had seemed really upset. . . .

But it didn't matter, really. She was the one who had started all this, and apologizing didn't change what she'd done. It didn't matter if I was cold. My note was direct and to the point. And I didn't really think I'd have to explain why I'd decided to work on my own.

The bell rang, and everyone scrambled up from their seats. I tore the page out of my notebook and folded it up, then grabbed my stuff and bolted from the room as quickly as possible. I had to get to Jessica's locker before she did.

I jogged down the hall, and when I got there, Jessica was nowhere in sight. With shaky fingers I slipped the note through one of the slots in her locker door and hurried away. As I headed for my next class, I realized I felt tired and kind of . . . broken. But I had to put it out of my head. My friendship with Jessica was over, but it didn't matter.

Who needed friends like her anyway?

Lila

I didn't go to school on Tuesday. The night before, after Jessica freaked out on me and I cried for like an hour straight, I couldn't fall asleep. It was awful. Every time I did finally doze off, I'd have a nightmare and wake up sweating. It happened about ten times. So by the time my alarm went off in the morning, I felt disgusting. Hester took one look at my pale face and the purple bags under my eyes and said it was okay for me to stay home. I was glad my dad was away on a business trip. He'd probably make me go to school if I was coughing up a lung.

I spent the whole day watching bad soap operas, reading magazines, and taking naps. By the time three o'clock rolled around, all I wanted to do was get out of the house and breathe some fresh air.

I pulled myself out of bed and took a shower. While I was in there, deep conditioning my hair, I thought about all the lame soap operas I'd seen that day. There was one little thing that could be learned from the crazy women on those shows. They stood up for themselves. They demanded respect. So what if some guy had ditched Bianca for her sister and stolen all of her money and run a front-page story claiming she was an alien? She wouldn't let anyone get away with running all over her.

That was a woman who knew how to handle herself.

By the time I was clean and feeling like myself again, I knew what I had to do. I was going to find Ashlee and make her tell me what had been going on with the Double E's lately.

This is ridiculous, I told myself as I brushed my hair out in front of the mirror in my room. *I'm Lila Fowler. I'm not a victim.* And I wasn't going to spend one more minute feeling like one. It was time for me to stand up for myself . . . just like Jessica had done the day before.

Dean, my dad's driver, pulled the car up in front of the Sweet Valley Swim Club just as Ashlee's diving practice was getting out. I told him I'd either walk home or call him if I needed him and hopped out of the car the second I saw Ashlee heading for the sidewalk.

"Thanks, Dean!" I said. Then I straightened

my skirt, pulled down on my T-shirt, and lifted my chin. It was do-or-die time.

"Ashlee!" I called out as I crossed the street.

She stopped and looked up. When she spotted me, she raised her eyebrows, obviously surprised to see me. I didn't blame her. Not only wasn't I in school that day, but I'd never even been to the swim club before in my life.

"Hi, Lila," she said a bit coolly. She adjusted her sports bag on her shoulder and squeezed some excess water out of her curls as I walked over. "Were you sick today?" she asked.

"Kind of," I said. "But that's not what I'm here to talk about."

She gave me a suspicious look and shifted her weight from one leg to the other. "What's up?" she asked, crossing her arms over her damp T-shirt.

"I want to know what's been going on with you guys lately," I said, trying not to sound nervous, even though I was—just a little. "Why have you and Courtnee and Maree been ditching me and acting so bratty all the time?"

Ashlee pulled back her chin and just looked at me for a second like she couldn't believe what I'd just said.

"*Us?*" she finally screeched. "What's been going on with *us* lately? Is this a joke? Am I on TV or something?" She looked around, pretending she was searching for a camera crew.

I felt my face turn bright red and glanced at a few people who had stopped to stare when Ashlee had her outburst. This wasn't a reaction I'd expected. I'd thought she would get all nervous and try to explain.

"Jeez, Lila, I don't know what planet you've been living on, but you're the one that's been acting like a brat," Ashlee fumed. "You're always ordering us around and expecting us to only do what you want to do. And then you act like the stuff we want to do isn't good enough for you. It's insulting!"

Ashlee's pale skin was turning almost purple behind her freckles. All I wanted was for her to calm down before she totally lost it. I couldn't handle being trashed by two best friends in two days.

"Ashlee—"

"No!" she said, holding up a hand to silence me. "As for ditching you, you're the one who's been acting like you're oh-so-cool with that whole movie thing you've been doing with Jessica Wakefield. If hanging out with her is so much cooler than hanging out with us, why do you even care what we've been doing for the past week?"

I was so stunned by what I was hearing, it took me a second to find my voice, but when I did, at least I had a comeback. I mean, what she was saying was totally unfair.

"I only started doing that project with Jessica because you guys kept making plans without me," I said, keeping my voice even. We didn't both need to be making a scene. "You guys bailed at my house to go see that movie, and then you didn't ask me to go to dinner that night when you totally could have called me . . . and then I bumped into you at the mall, and that was *before* you knew about the documentary."

Ashlee looked down at the ground and adjusted her bag again. I knew I had her. I was right about those things, and there was nothing she could say.

"Look, we really wanted to see the movie that day, and we thought we could do both—go to your house and to the movie," Ashlee said slowly. "And if you want to know about the mall, we didn't invite you because of the way you acted at your house."

"What do you mean?" I asked, confused.

"All that stuff about Courtnee needing new eyes and Maree needing to chop off her hair," Ashlee said, looking me in the eye. "Plus you were so moody and negative at the slumber party last week. . . . You act like you're so great all the time. Maybe we wanted to go to the mall and not have you telling us how bad we looked in the stuff we liked and directing us about what to buy."

Ashlee turned around and plopped down on a wooden bench just off the sidewalk. She took a deep breath and concentrated on picking her nails. I was just trying to process everything she'd said.

"What were we supposed to do, Lila?" she said finally. "Follow you around like puppy dogs for the rest of our lives?"

When she said that, I felt a pang right in the middle of my heart. Everything she'd just spilled sounded eerily familiar—it sounded a lot like everything Jessica had said the day before.

I sighed and sat down next to her, feeling like a total jerk. "When you put it that way . . . I sound like a complete idiot," I said, releasing a small laugh. Ashlee laughed too, but she was still staring at her nails. "I'm really sorry," I said honestly. "I guess I should try not to be so . . . controlling. I didn't mean to hurt anyone's feelings."

Of course, it seemed like that was *all* I had been doing lately.

"It's okay," Ashlee said, finally looking up at me. "I mean, *Time and Time Again* really wasn't as good the second time." She smiled. "Of course, Maree and Courtnee want to see it again!"

I rolled my eyes and smiled. "You have to be kidding."

"Nope," Ashlee said. She shook her head and grinned at me. "So, friends?"

"Friends," I answered with a nod. I was so relieved, I leaned over and hugged her, but it wasn't a totally dorky moment because she hugged me back. "Let's go get some ice cream," I said, standing.

"Cool," Ashlee responded. "So, how's the documentary going anyway?" she asked as we started off toward Scoops.

I sighed and closed my eyes. There was someone else I needed to apologize to. . . .

Elizabeth's Journal

Okay, something is definitely wrong with my sister.

First of all, she skipped track practice, which she never does. Second, she came straight home from school, grabbed an apple, and disappeared. I couldn't even figure out where she was until Steven got home from his friend's house and found her locked up in his room, using his stereo, VCR, and microphone. When he told her to get out, she told _him_ to get out, and he _did_! She has to be possessed or something if Steven's letting her kick him out of his own room.

Unless something's wrong with him too.

Anyway, I know our project is due tomorrow, but I thought Jessica had finished it. Now she's spending a beautiful afternoon—when she could be running with the team or at least sunning herself by the pool—locked in Steven's dingy room?

She's either delirious or . . .

Nope. She must be delirious.

Bethel

On Wednesday morning I was sitting in history class, wishing I were anywhere else in the world. I would have gladly stayed home and cleaned the bathroom with a toothbrush if it meant I could miss this torture. Part of me knew I should be paying attention as the other kids in class presented their projects. But I was too distracted. All I could think about was the stupid paper I'd written at the last minute. Not only was Harriman going to flunk me, but I actually deserved the F.

As Elizabeth, Salvador, and Anna presented their absolutely beautiful Sweet Valley board game, I stared at the typed pages in front of me. Everyone else had done such cool projects. I was dreading getting up there and trying to present this thing. Maybe I could fake a stomach cramp and bolt for the door.

"Thank you, Elizabeth, Anna, and Salvador," Mr. Harriman said as the class clapped. "You've done a lovely job."

As my friends smiled and took their seats, I prayed Mr. Harriman would forget I was in the room. Hey, it was possible. The guy once forgot to wear a sock. One sock.

"Next we'll hear from Jessica Wakefield and Bethel McCoy," Mr. Harriman said, reading off his list.

My stomach turned as Jessica started to stand up from the desk next to mine. I grabbed her arm before she could get all the way out of her chair.

"You didn't tell him we weren't working together?" I hissed.

"That's okay, Bethel," Jessica said in a loud voice, exaggerating a smile. "I'll start the tape."

Before I could say anything else, she'd walked to the front of the room and popped her project into the VCR. Mr. Harriman turned off the lights and turned on the TV, causing the big, blue screen to send a freakish glow over the room. My heart was slamming against my chest. My name was going to be on a project that wasn't even supposed to be mine anymore. I couldn't believe this was happening.

Jessica pressed play and returned to her desk. I didn't even look at her. I couldn't pull my eyes away from the screen, like it was a speeding train bearing down on me and I was too scared to move.

A wide shot of the school came up on the screen, and then Jessica's voice was heard saying, "SVJH—a Documentary. By Bethel McCoy and Jessica Wakefield."

I rolled my eyes, trying to look like I wasn't remotely interested in what she'd done. Then Jessica was on camera, standing in front of the lockers. This was footage I'd never seen before. She must have shot it with Elizabeth or Damon or something.

"There are a lot of things that I think define life in junior high today," Jessica said, in a perfect reporter's tone.

"Like gross food . . ." The image changed to a shot I'd taken of Salvador eating a sloppy joe, then making a horrified face and covering his mouth with a napkin. The class cracked up.

"Not wanting to go to class . . . ," Jessica continued. There was a shot of Kristin rolling her eyes as the announcements were made in homeroom.

"Competitive after-school sports . . ." There were a few shots of the football team practicing and Tommy jogging over to us, lifting off his helmet. Too cute.

"Bad excuses for missed homework . . ." Then Larissa was on-screen, telling her math teacher that she hadn't had time to do her homework because she'd forgotten to switch her clock back to standard time. The class laughed again. I couldn't help smiling, remembering how Jessica and I had caught that moment on tape.

"But I think the most important thing to the kids at Sweet Valley Junior High today is the same thing that's most important to anyone, anywhere, of any age," Jessica continued as the tape switched from shot to shot of people in the halls, acting like goofs, gossiping, and going over homework.

"And that's friendship," Jessica said.

Now there was a montage of images set to music. There were all of my friends playing Frisbee, Brian and Blue wrestling jokingly in gym class, Kristin and Lacey leaning over a table, obviously in deep conversation. Anna, Salvador, and Toby laughing, the silly shot of Damon and Jessica fake kissing, Blue giving Elizabeth a piggyback ride down the hall while Elizabeth laughed uncontrollably.

And then there was a shot of Jessica and me at track practice. I pulled Jessica's ponytail, and she laughed and chased me down the track. I felt another threat of tears.

"Friendship is universal," Jessica said over the footage. "It doesn't matter what year you're living in or how old you are. Whether you're eight years old or eighty, your friends are the ones

who make you laugh, who make you cry, who
make mistakes, who are there for you—even
when you feel like you don't deserve them.
Friendship is what life today is all about. We
hope it always will be."

The video ended on a shot of all of our
friends waving at the camera, and Jessica had
somehow put it in slow motion as it panned
over everyone's faces. I had to admit, it was really cool. And I was definitely . . . touched.

The whole class applauded and turned
around to congratulate us. Mr. Harriman loudly
blew his nose, and it was obvious the poor guy
was trying not to cry. He got up and flicked on
the lights, blinding everyone in the room.

"Beautiful, girls," he said. "Just beautiful. I'm
very proud of this project."

As the bell rang, Jessica just glanced at me
and sort of half smiled. I was too stunned to
even respond as she hurried out of the room.

I grabbed my books, shoved them in my bag,
and took off after her. I knew I had to say something. Hopefully by the time I caught up with
her, I'd figure out exactly what it should be.

Jessica

"Jess, that was so cool!" Elizabeth exclaimed as we walked down the hall. "I can't believe how great it looked."

"It was totally professional," Salvador agreed, shrugging into his backpack. "Of course, I think you could have used *me* a little bit more. I mean, not to be egotistical or anything, but I think I gave you some really good material and—"

I rolled my eyes and laughed. "Don't push it, Sal," I said, glancing around. My hands were still shaking from nerves, and I was wondering where Bethel was and what she was thinking.

"Besides, your reaction to the sloppy joe did get the biggest laugh," Anna put in, patting him on the back.

Salvador rolled his shoulders back, looking very proud of himself. "Yeah, it did, didn't it?" he said. "I'm a star."

"Ugh!" Elizabeth groaned, grabbing his arm. She looked at Anna. "We better get him out of here before his head explodes." Anna laughed and grabbed his other arm, and together they pulled him off down the hall.

"No autographs, people, no autographs!" Salvador called out, even though no one was paying any attention to him. He was still blabbing as Anna and Elizabeth jostled him into the stairwell.

I shook my head and laughed as I continued down the hall. At least the whole thing was over and done with. Mr. Harriman had liked the documentary, and Bethel hadn't freaked out on me. Still, I was going to have to face her at some point, and I guess that was why part of me was still nervous. I shoved my hands into the front pockets of my jeans and tried to chill out.

"Jessica!"

My heart dropped the second I heard Bethel call me, and I kept walking, pretending I hadn't heard. Apparently I wasn't ready to face her just yet. What if she was really mad and going to yell at me in the middle of the hall? That was something I definitely couldn't deal with at that moment.

"Jess! Wait up!"

I could tell she was getting closer, so I stopped. There was no use in trying to get away from Bethel anyway. She was faster than I was, even in a crowded hallway. I took a deep breath and turned around.

Jessica

"Hey," Bethel said, stopping in front of me.

"Hey," I said.

We both just sort of stood there and looked away, waiting for the other person to talk. It was one of the most uncomfortable silences I've ever experienced.

"So," she said.

"So," I repeated.

We glanced at each other, and I couldn't take it anymore. "Okay, this has to stop," I said. Bethel cracked a small smile, and I stepped closer to the wall to get out of the way of all the people rushing to class. Bethel followed.

"Listen, I don't expect you to forgive me," I said, my heart still skipping ridiculously quickly. "That's not why I made that tape. I just want you to know how sorry I am, and I hope what I said in the documentary proved that."

Bethel leaned one shoulder against the wall. She still looked angry, but not as angry as the day before. She didn't have that cold, hard look in her eyes that had hurt me so much when we were walking to school. My pulse started to calm down a little.

"I know you're sorry," she said. "I guess you're right—all friends make mistakes. . . . Of course, they usually aren't as huge, rude, and hurtful as the mistake you made, but that's not important right now." She cracked a smile, and I grinned back. At least she was joking with me again.

"I have an idea!" she said, pushing herself away from the wall and placing her hands on her hips. "How about neither one of us ever makes a mistake like that again?"

"Deal," I said, sticking out my hand.

"Deal," Bethel said. We shook on it and started to walk down the hall.

"Good work on the documentary, Jess. Harriman was all over it," Bethel said as she shuffled along, her new sneakers squeaking on the linoleum floor. "I'm glad you didn't take my name off it."

I smiled. "Yeah. We did a really great job," I said, glancing at her out of the corner of my eye.

Bethel didn't look over, but she was trying hard not to smile. "Yeah. We really did."

"I swear, I overheard Mr. Harriman telling Ms. McGuire about your project, and they're thinking about showing it to the whole school," Elizabeth told me, practically skipping into the house on Wednesday after school.

"You're such a liar," I said, closing the door behind us. But my face was burning with excitement. Elizabeth had been talking about this all the way home, and I knew she hadn't made it up. For one, why would she? And second, Elizabeth wasn't a liar by nature.

"Just don't be surprised if we have an assembly tomorrow," Elizabeth said as we dropped our bags in the living room and headed for the kitchen like we did every day. She pulled her ponytail holder from her hair and shook back her hair. "I hope Mom went shopping."

"I know," I replied, stretching my arms over my head. "There's never anything good in the kitchen."

We walked through the door and stopped in our tracks. There, sitting at the table with our mom, was Lila. What was *she* doing here?

"Hi, girls," my mom said, smirking as she stood up. "Jessica, Lila's here to see you . . . and I did go shopping, but I can't guarantee I got anything good."

"Hi, guys," Lila said, standing.

"Hey," Elizabeth and I said at the same time in the same flat tone.

My mom crossed the room and put her arm around Elizabeth's shoulders. "Honey, why don't you grab something to eat and come join me in the den?"

"Okay," Elizabeth said, shooting me an encouraging look. She grabbed a bag of chocolate-chip cookies from the counter and followed my mom out of the room.

I glanced at Lila and immediately felt a twinge of guilt for being so hard on her on Monday. I knew I had taken out my frustration about what had happened with Bethel on her, and it wasn't entirely Lila's fault. Bethel was right. I hadn't said anything to defend her, and that was my mistake, not Lila's.

"Look, you were pretty harsh the other day," Lila said, fiddling with the hem of her cardigan. "And I still can't believe you said some of the things you said . . . but you were partially right."

I blinked. She couldn't have actually just said that. "I was?"

"Partially," Lila repeated, leveling me with a reproachful look. "I can be kind of a jerk sometimes." She sighed and crossed her arms over her chest, staring at the floor. I knew she was having a hard time. Lila almost never apologizes, and as long as I'd known her, I couldn't remember her *ever* admitting she was wrong. Not even in fifth grade when she'd mixed plaids with polka dots.

She finally lifted her head and looked me in the eyes. "So, I hope we can still be friends," she said. "I mean, I think I can act like an actual *friend* if you . . . you know . . . give me a chance."

I felt this warm sort of feeling spread through

147

my heart and smiled. I knew Lila wasn't going to change overnight, but the fact that she was going to try was enough for me.

"We're still friends," I said with a smile. "We always will be."

Lila smiled back. "You know, when we get to Sweet Valley High, maybe we really will rule the school."

"Yeah," I said with a laugh. "Maybe we will."

I walked Lila to the door and gave her a little hug before saying good-bye. As I watched her stroll off toward her house, I felt sort of proud of myself. Not only had I stood up to Lila, but I knew now that Bethel and I would be okay.

I'd finally realized who my real friends were, and knowing that made me feel a little bit . . . older . . . somehow.

And that felt really good.

Lila's Journal

You'll never believe where I'm going tonight. I'm going to see Time and Time Again. Again! Maree and Courtnee would not let the subject drop, so Ashlee and I finally caved and said we would go one more time. But they have to buy the popcorn.

Yes, my friends are insane, but they're cool. I really do have a good time with them, even when we're seeing movies for the second or third time.

Plus we're going to be doing something a little different next weekend. My dad felt so guilty that he was away while I was "sick," he got us tickets to this huge charity fashion show in LA next weekend, and he's having Dean drive us and everything. There are even going to be celebrities there! (Maybe the people that made Time and Time Again will show, and I can tell them exactly how much their movie stinks.)

Anyway, I'm thinking about asking Jessica to come with us. Now that we're friends again. She could even bring that Bethel girl. She could use a good fashion show.

Bethel's Journal

Jessica's on her way over to help me baby-sit my little cousins. Hey, I didn't ask her — the girl offered. She has no idea what she's in for. I think she fell in love with the little psychos at the barbecue, but she didn't get to see what they're <u>really</u> like. I love them, but I can only save the cat from getting sheared so many times.

I think Jessica volunteered because she feels like she has to make up for what she did. And to be honest, I kind of think she does. She's not out of the doghouse yet. But it was nice of her to sacrifice a Saturday afternoon to sit inside with me and watch Barney videos. Jessica really is a good friend. Of course, I may not tell her that until after she changes a few diapers.

Uh . . . I have to go. The doorbell just rang, and the kids must have answered it. I think I hear Jessica screaming. . . .

Maybe I'll tell her what a good friend she is <u>right</u> <u>now</u>.

You hate your **alarm clock.**

You hate your **clothes.**

You're going to love Jr. High.